THE MAN

WHO CAME

AND WENT

THE MAN WHO CAME AND WENT

A Novel By

JOE STILLMAN

City Point Press

CITY POINT PRESS 2022

City Point Press

P.O. Box 2063

Westport, CT 06880

www.citypointpress.com

(203) 571-0781

Hardcover ISBN 978-1-947951-38-9

eBook ISBN 978-1-947951-39-6

Book and cover design by Barbara Aronica-Buck

Cover illustration by Susan Stillman; a composite of images by Warren Wong / unsplash.com, Wikimedia, and Juan /pexels.com.

This is a work of fiction. Names, characters, business, events and incidents are the products of the author's imagination. Any resemblance to actual persons, living or dead, or actual events is purely coincidental.

Manufactured in the United States

To my two sisters:
Susan Stillman, whom I've been lucky enough
to have in my life since it started,
and Michele Russell, my acquired sister and
North Star for this project at times my compass failed.

Before I can start this story, I have to tell you something that happened near the end of it. I'm sorry if that seems weird, but believe me you're going to be really glad I did this.

We were on the road to Phoenix, the five of us. I was sitting in the middle of the back seat. Bill was to my right, looking out the window. Rodney was to my left, lost in thought and silent. Silence was a new experience for Rodney and I have to say it was a vast improvement. I made a mental note to suggest he try it more often.

Maybell was in the front seat driving. Rose was next to her. Both of them stared at the road ahead. No one was talking. Really, what was there to say after what happened?

We were in Rose's car, a white Ford Escort. We thought about taking Martin's Oldsmobile Cutlass because it was bigger. I really think he would have liked that. But we had already broken enough laws that day, and it was time to get Bill where he needed to go.

I'm not sure how long we had been riding in silence. Long enough so that the hum of the car became the only sound in the world. I was alone in my thoughts, replaying what happened, trying to make sense of it. And then suddenly, I wasn't anymore. Alone, I mean. Bill was in there with me, in my thoughts, in my head, talking to me.

I had never known until that moment what a sanctuary my thoughts had been. It was the one place in the entire universe that belonged only to me. What a beautiful and terrible thing that is, to have such isolation.

I didn't exactly hear Bill's voice. There wasn't any sound. It was more like a sense of his thinking, which happened to be right next to my own.

My first reaction was panic. Blind panic, if you really want to know. Who wouldn't be scared? It felt like being naked in your bed in the middle of the night when suddenly the lights go on and you realize the whole world is in there with you.

The whole world wasn't inside my head. But if one person could just come and go willy-nilly, then the very idea of privacy was suddenly blown to pieces. In that moment, reality as I understood it had ended. At the same time, a new and different reality, one that was completely foreign, opened up before me.

My heart was beating like a jackhammer.

I will say that, to Bill's credit, he knew how to calm me down. I don't know how many times he had done this before, or with how many people, but he was pretty matter-of-fact. He let me know he had something he wanted to tell me, something that couldn't be said in words or sentences. I didn't understand at the time, but I do now. The process of speaking—thought to mouth to ear—was all too clumsy. I had never thought of it before as being slow, but Bill had. He said talking was a bit like analog, and what he had to get across to me was more like digital. It was big and complex and could only be imparted directly to my mind.

And that's what he did. Thoughts came faster than I knew they could. Scary fast. It would have all been completely nonsensical if Bill hadn't told me how to take it in. By the time he was done, after Bill had imparted everything he came to say, I finally knew all there was to know.

I knew the story of Bill.

I knew the story of Maybell and Rose and Martin and pretty much everyone around us.

I knew things I couldn't know.

About people I didn't know.

About things that, until that moment, I would have thought impossible to know.

The point I'm trying to get across here is that in one very powerful explosion of thought, I knew pretty much the whole story.

Now I can start. . . .

I heard the truck pulling in just after midnight. Some nights Maybell would come back with a guy. Some nights not at all. Sometimes Marguerite would drop her off if the pickings were slim. Tonight it was a Ford pickup, an engine I hadn't heard before.

The engine cut out. A truck door slammed. Then another closed very slowly. I knew why. Maybell was drunk and having trouble getting out. After that, there was silence. I knew what that meant too. She and the guy were making out on the side of his truck. Maybell liked to get her foreplay out of the way outside.

On the way out the front door, I picked up my rifle. It had once belonged to Maybell's father, who died a year before I was born. Maybell had no use for it and even at a young age I was a natural shot. So it pretty much became mine. In my other hand I held a mug that said, "World's Worst Mother." I had it specially made. The tea inside, like the love I once had for Maybell, had gone cold.

I could hear Maybell from the guy's truck. "Shh, you don't wanna wake my daughter."

The guy had Maybell against the truck, one hand on her breast, the other trying to squeeze its way into her too-tight jeans. If he saw how she bent the laws of physics to get into those jeans, he probably would have let them be.

None of her conquests had names to me. I called them all Jerkoff Du Jour. I know there are those who excuse guys when they're only out for sex. It is, after all, just biology. Like dogs in heat, they're hostage to the primal grip of lust. And once they get their leg-humping out of the way, they can go back to their more civilized selves: fixing your car or teaching your kids math. I get all that. The problem is, I've seen these guys at their worst. That's what Maybell brings out in them. A dog will eventually give you love or loyalty. Maybe fetch a stick. Every guy Maybell brought home would take his sex and go.

Earlier that night, I had left my bedroom in time to see Maybell reaching for the front door. She was wearing those jeans I mentioned and a dungaree blouse tied above her navel to show off her midriff. Her hair, naturally dark, was colored her favorite shade of blonde. Though her back was to me, I could practically hear her breasts sloshing around. She was dressed for sex and there was not a man in Hadley who wouldn't be eating out of her hand.

By the time I got outside, Maybell had reached the passenger side of Marguerite's truck. Marguerite could always handle her beer and was the designated driver.

"Where do you think you're going?" I said to Maybell. The question was rhetorical. They were off to her favorite bar.

She turned back to me. "You're gonna make a fine mother one day."

"You sure didn't!"

Marguerite rolled down her window and called: "Hey, Belutha!"

I had nothing against Marguerite, but she was enabling my mom and you can't reward that kind of behavior.

I pointed my finger. "I want her back by eleven!"

Maybell got in, and I heard the two of them giggling like teenagers.

Marguerite put the truck in reverse and Maybell rolled down the window. "Don't wait up! That's an order!"

The truck pivoted over the desert gravel and took off with a roar.

About an hour later, Sonny Boy sugar-crashed and crawled off to bed without brushing his teeth. I used to be on him about that, but lately I figured he was old enough to face the consequences of his own failures. He was thirteen and spent all his non–school time playing video games or eating food, usually at the same time. That left him about twenty pounds overweight and completely antisocial. He wasn't a bad guy. It's just that living in that house had turned him in on himself, and it was hard to know if he was ever going to come out.

I had put Clover down around nine o'clock, but like clockwork he woke up at eleven-thirty, crying for a feeding. Even when Maybell was home, it was usually me who mixed the formula and gave Clover the bottle. Actual breast milk was out of the question, of course. Those globes hanging from Maybell's chest had no domestic utility. For someone who had no qualms about reproducing, Maybell possessed a complete lack of any maternal instinct.

With Clover out again and Sonny Boy asleep, and with Maybell off to the ruin of all, the place was finally quiet. It was the only time that I felt I belonged there. I held my tea and had an open schoolbook on my lap. But I wasn't reading it. The quiet was too precious and had to be savored.

Maybell's house was actually a trailer with another half-trailer added to it, because that's how Maybell lived—putting things together that didn't belong. Like me and Sonny Boy. Two kids with different fathers: both assholes. And Clover, her latest mistake—another father and, I have to think, probably another asshole. None of us knew who the guy was. Some trucker on a long haul passing through, we figured.

Clover was eight months old now. When Maybell was pregnant with him, she made it clear that, since she'd be working full-time at the diner, the burden of caring for this new baby was going to fall on me. I became determined that I would hate that thing growing inside her. But on the day Clover was born, I held him in my arms and he melted me. He was one hundred percent innocent of any crime committed by our mother. I decided then that he should be kept carefree and unburdened by the family he was born into for as long as possible.

The problem was that I pretty much had to raise him, more than I had done with Sonny Boy. Maybell was off to the diner at five-thirty, so every morning I would wake up with Clover, change him, feed him, burp him, dress him, then drop him off at the diner before going to school. Sometimes I'd pick him up on the way home. If not, I'd usually hit the P&Q and load up on supplies for him and the rest of us. Of course I'd babysit at night while Maybell went out looking to hook up with another guy and start that tragic cycle all over again.

All that would end soon, at least for me. This was the year I'd be graduating high school. I'd be gone from that house and that town and that mother. I'd be gone and I'd never look back.

When I stepped outside, I saw tonight's Jerkoff slurping at Maybell like she was a happy hour drink. He was younger than her by about fifteen years, pretty trim, with a full head of close-cropped hair. I'd tell you that Maybell liked them young, but that wasn't true. She liked them breathing.

Jerkoff would have done Maybell right on the side of the truck. Standing, lying down, the problem of gravity was of no concern to a man's lizard brain. But Maybell preferred the ceremony of a bed and motioned toward the house. That's when Jerkoff turned and saw me standing in the doorway.

"Who's this," he asked. "Yer little girl?"

Maybell leaned back against the truck for support. "Oh, Lord. Belutha, honey, this is . . ." She tried to remember Jerkoff's name.

"Henry," Jerkoff said. He sauntered up to me like he was still on the hunt in a bar. "Belutha, huh? That's a pretty name. Pretty name for a pretty girl."

Maybell shook her head. "Oh, my—" She knew where this was going.

"You and your mom, you like ta do everything together?" Jerkoff gave me a leer in case there was some chance I didn't know he meant sex.

I have to say that was a low, even for a jerkoff. He was leaning so close I could smell the bar on his breath and clothes. I didn't think through what happened next. My body acted on its own. I was very proud of it.

I threw the cold tea in his face and suddenly shouted: "HOT COFFEE!"

Jerkoff screamed and fell back about ten feet. In fairness, I suppose the power of suggestion works marvels on a drunken mind, and the sensation of cold can sometimes seem hot.

"Daaaaaaam! Fuuuuuuck!!" He touched his face and realized it wasn't burned. "What the fuck?! Is your bitch daughter crazy?!"

Now I was back on plan. I lifted my rifle.

"Shh! Ya hear that? Coyote!" I fired and hit the ground about two feet from Jerkoff.

"Jesus Christ!" he yelled.

I pretended I heard something else. "Look, there's another one." This time I hit a rock between his legs.

"Jesus, Maybell! Jesus!" Jerkoff ran to his truck.

"Don't you come around here no more, mister!" I yelled at him. "We got enough babies in this house."

His truck peeled out. Maybell was wobbly without something to lean against. I put my arm around her waist to lead her inside.

"Let's get you to bed, Maybell."

"That's the right line," she said, stumbling next to me. "But you're the wrong guy."

H adley was less of a town and more a placeholder where someone eventually intended a town to be. It was located in an empty corner of Arizona, a place you didn't want to live if you had a choice of living anywhere else. There was a post office, a police station, some banks, a couple of churches, a sad excuse for a public school, and one main street with a few pointless stores. Maybell's diner was the only place to get yourself a meal, if you didn't count the mini-mart at the Chevron station. Most of us didn't.

The nearest town with anything worthwhile was Gaylordville. They had a mall and also a grocery store called the P&Q, where you might find an actual vegetable if you went on the right day.

A bus connected the two towns. It was the same bus that came out from Phoenix. Hadley was the last stop on the line, and I like to think that whoever decided on that understood where I lived. It was the last place you wanted to be.

It was that bus that brought Bill to our town. How that happened, I'll get into soon. Right now, this is about what happened when he got off the bus.

Maybell was having a typical day at the diner. I should probably tell you that while Maybell hadn't quite reached her expiration date, she was definitely beyond her use-by date. By that I mean she was well past the age most women have settled down with a man who's legally bound to not give a shit how they wind up looking. Still, Maybell remained what most guys consider luscious. She was tall and striking, with movie star cheekbones. Even rounding forty, her blue eyes could freeze a man to his seat. The desert sun hadn't been terribly kind to her skin, but it hadn't been altogether mean. And no matter what outfit she wore, her boobs spilled forth this way and that, a quality that never seemed to lose its allure. That spillage didn't happen by accident. Maybell positioned her breasts for maximum impact. They swung like a watch on a chain, hypnotizing any man who came within range. If it were up to me, I'd have covered them with something permanent, like plywood or sheet metal. This way they couldn't cause any more damage.

Maybell had always been able to get any guy in Hadley. The problem was, nothing ever took. I was okay with that. The selection in town was pretty grim.

That day, the day Bill arrived, my mom was serving up eggs and complaints.

"Dammit, that daughter 'a mine," she yelled to Dolene, across the diner. "She's like walking birth control. Does she think I'm trying to have babies? Scuse me, Darlin." Maybell gave Clover's bubble walker a little kick, sending it between tables 4 and 6 so she could get by and dump a load of dishes behind the counter.

Dolene was homegrown, like the tumbleweed, with eyes like a golden retriever that never quite looked at you directly. She was smart enough to add up a check, but you could tell she was never getting out of Hadley. "I take it you didn't get laid last night."

Maybell pointed to her sour puss. "Does this say 'laid' to you?"

There was a "harrumph" from booth 5 by the window. That was Rose. Rose was an old woman by the time she was thirty. Now she was in her late sixties, a widow since before I was born—in other words, forever. She liked to spend her afternoons at Maybell's Diner, reading her book and keeping an eye on the goings on around her, as if she was the town's homeroom teacher.

"Look at Saint Rose," Maybell said, stuffing dirty plates into the plastic tub under the counter. "Thinks she smells better than Mentos. I ain't running a library here, Rose. Next time bring *Reader's Digest*!"

There was another sound from Rose, something between a "well" and a "pfffft." She never took her eyes off her book.

The door opened with a *ding!* from the bell that hung on it. No one noticed Bill entering. He was about average in height, but his skinny frame made him look taller. You could tell from his face that he was in his mid-twenties, but those were hard years he had lived, and his body looked frail and geriatric. His clothes were old and clung to him like an extra layer of skin, with a smell that would never wash out.

The angles of his face were sharp and careworn. But his eyes, those were different. His face was hard and weathered, but his eyes were soft. They seemed brand new.

No one in the diner even looked. If they did they would have seen those eyes taking in every little detail: the people talking, forks carrying food, the string lights behind the counter, Dolene ringing up a check. But what drew Bill more than anything else was the grill. Harley, the grill cook, must have had four meals going at once, each with its own set of sounds and smells. Most of those meals involved eggs. His spatula made a metal-on-metal scrape as he turned them. Bill was riveted. He went to sit at the counter to watch.

Down the counter, a porkish-looking man named Earle—probably one of three men in town who had never slept with my mom—raised his empty cup. "Can I get a refill, Maybell?"

Maybell stopped and faced him. "Seriously, Earle? Is it so goddam much trouble for you to get up off your ass and get it yourself? Can't you see I'm working here?"

"Well . . ." he stammered. "I just—was I—I was—"

Maybell pointed to the coffee pot. "How far away is that? Two feet?"

"Sure, I guess . . ."

"Am I your personal slave, Earle? Is that why God put me on earth?"

"No, I don't think you're—"

Maybell grabbed the pot and sloshed coffee in his cup. "There. You happy now?"

He nodded meekly.

While she had the pot in her hand, Maybell filled the cup sitting in front of Bill. "I'll be by to take your order in a minute, hon."

Maybell walked on. Bill just sat there and stared at the coffee. For him, there was no diner anymore, no Maybell, no clanking dishes or dumb conversation. He leaned closer to that cup like it was the only thing in the world. And there he was, smelling coffee for the first time. And it smelled like life. Like a whole world. Like this is how a planet smells if you're up in space and could take a deep breath. Bill was motionless for who knows how long. And then, when he was good and ready, he took his first sip.

Those eyes, the ones that didn't belong in his head, they closed as if he was praying. No, more like he was hearing a prayer. The coffee was praying to be heard, and Bill heard it. He only opened his eyes when someone shouted nearby. It was Harley, the grill cook.

"Dammit, May, you haven't given me an answer!"

"Harley, would you give it a rest!"

"No, I will not give it a rest. I will not be . . . dissuaded. You cannot dissuade me, Maybell!" When Harley got mad, he spoke in three-syllable words because he believed they made him sound smarter.

Harley was Maybell's age and they had known each other since first grade. If he didn't work the grill at Maybell's Diner, he'd probably be spending his days on the other side of the counter, nursing bottomless cups of coffee, complaining about how unfair life was to him. In truth, life wasn't in the business of giving people like Harley a lot of breaks.

"People come here ta eat my cooking," he shouted. "That means I got draw power. I'm like your Dwayne Johnson. You know how much that guy makes?"

Maybell was busy taking someone's order. Harley frowned and went back to cooking.

While Bill was somewhere around his second or third sip, a guy named Radd sat down two seats from him. Radd was a slight, graying man in his late fifties who never did anybody harm. He worked at a machine shop over in Gaylordville. Sometimes he smelled like old man, but I liked him.

"Mornin', Harley," Radd said, taking his usual seat at the counter. "What's going on?"

"Same shit. Same day," Harley said with a bite. "What'll you have?"

"Scramble two."

Harley cracked open two eggs and spun them around in a metal bowl using two forks. Bill stared in fascination, his coffee momentarily forgotten. In one gesture, Harley oiled the grill and poured out the mixture with a metal clang, fork and bowl hitting the grill. He turned back to Maybell.

"Still waitin', Maybell!"

"Harley, just leave it alone!"

Radd shook his head. "Damn, Harley, you still on about a raise? Don't take this hard, but you ain't ever cooked an egg right in your life."

Harley pointed a stern finger. "I don't need shit from you, Radd!"

Radd went on. "Scrambled eggs, you don't just leave 'em on the grill and flip 'em once like a burger. They need care and attention."

Harley held his spatula like it was a lethal weapon. People who ate at Maybell's Diner sometimes felt like it was. He looked down at the grill and shouted at Maybell, as if she were simmering next to Radd's eggs. "I want a raise or I quit!"

Maybell shook her head. "Harley, you shut up or I'll quit."

Bill was so fascinated by this exchange, he didn't notice Radd until the old man leaned right up to his face.

"Now look at those eggs Mister," Radd said to Bill. "He's gonna leave 'em there ta get all hard."

Curious now, Bill looked at the eggs. Having the two men assessing his work was more than Harley could stomach. He slammed his spatula on the grill.

"Goddammit all, Maybell! I quit!"

Harley pulled off his apron and threw it on the floor. I'm thinking he had to be disappointed by the muffled, non-sound it made. He marched out the front door, with only a little *ding!* from the tiny bell to punctuate his indignation.

"Aw shit, Harley! Shit!" Maybell put down the dishes she was clearing and sped off after him.

Bill and Radd exchanged a look. Bill could tell what Radd was thinking, and they turned together to look at his eggs.

"See? Just leaves 'em there. Eggs is supposed to be stirred."

Bill looked at Radd's furrowed brow. Maybe Bill looked deep into Radd's soul, feeling the old man's need and his hunger. It's hard to be sure. But here's what did happen. Bill got up off his stool and went around behind the counter. He gave the eggs a stir, just in time. He grabbed some white toast that had just popped up and laid butter and then jam on it. He was about to slice it straight down the middle and then thought a moment and went diagonal. He reached for the home fries, the ones way in back that were good and crispy, and laid them on the plate along with the eggs. And then he turned and gave the plate to Radd.

The old man stared at the steam rising from his potatoes, the jam blending into the melted butter on his toast. Radd moved the soft eggs with his fork and then with that same fork gave his crispy home fries an audible tap-tap. He looked up at Bill and for a moment their eyes were very much alike, not quite matching the rest of their chiseled faces.

Maybell came marching back into the diner, alone. She was all business now.

"Dolene, honey, you're gonna be on your own for lunch. I'll be cooking. Let people help themselves to silver and coffee."

Maybell had already picked up a spare apron from under the counter and turned to the grill, when she found Bill standing in her way. She stopped short and blinked—one of the few times in her life she could think of nothing to say.

From the other side of the counter, Radd broke the silence. "Sonofabitch. Sonofa mother-truckin' bitch!" Radd held up a forkful of eggs. "These are good eggs, mister, and that's a fact."

Bill looked at Radd and smiled. He seemed glad to see Radd dig back in for more.

Maybell was still taking this in when Dolene stepped up and read from her pad: "Got a Western omelet takes fries. Steak and eggs special all the way." Dolene ripped out the check and put it on the spindle.

Snapping out of her daze, Maybell turned to Bill.

"I'll give you twenty-five bucks if you get me through lunch."

"The laws of where and when don't really matter all that much when you're not bound to a planet. They're a factor, sure. But they're also not a factor."
—Bill Bill, Interview at Maybell's Diner

Bill came out from the back dressed in kitchen whites. He looked lost, like a patient wandering around a hospital, unable to find his room. His apron strings dangled behind him. Maybell came up to tie them and led him to the grill.

"There's your eggs, your bacon, your meat, your pancake batter. Bread's there. Plates over there. Dolene and me take care of condiments and such." She plucked an order off the spindle. "Western omelet, steak 'n eggs." She pointed to a drawer by the grill. "Western mix in there. Cheese in the cold bin."

By the time Bill looked up from the cold bin, Maybell was gone.

She went to take an order from a local couple. But her mind was still on the grill. She saw Bill staring at it, not moving. Seconds were passing and she began to wonder if she had made a mistake. For all she knew, he was a psycho. She didn't like that big knife sitting on the narrow cutting board just to his right.

Maybell went behind the cash register and opened the utility drawer. There were extra pads and pens, aspirin, a first aid kit and various junk. Under the pile she found her handgun. She waited and kept her eye on Bill's right hand.

Bill told me later what was going on for him.

The grill was completely empty, on a pause between two cooks. It was quiet and almost pristine, but at the same time radiating heat and alive with possibility. It felt to him like a new planet, ready for whatever life was coming.

As he reached for the knife, Maybell wrapped her hand around the gun. Then, with his other hand Bill peeled off two slices of American cheese, which he cut into strips. He broke three eggs into the metal bowl and mixed them with two forks, like he had watched Harley doing. He poured the mixture onto the grill with that same metal clang, bowl and forks. And he laid the cheese on top.

Maybell let go of the gun and eased her hand out of the drawer, sliding it shut with her hip. She grabbed a pot of coffee to go give refills. As far as she was concerned, it was now just another day.

Maybell's Diner never got much more than half full, and that day it was a little on the light side. By around one-thirty, lunch was winding down. Maybell and Dolene hadn't noticed, but there was a different quality to the place.

People weren't talking as much. It's not that anyone who chose to live in Hadley had much worth saying. To my mind they just regurgitated the same dumb stuff day in and day out, as if they were all in a play and had to fill the time. But not that day. Not at Maybell's. People seemed more thoughtful and quiet. I think if you could put a microphone inside their heads, even their brains would have been quieter.

There was a quality to the food that was also different. Let's face it, there's only so many ways you can make grilled cheese or hamburgers. It was the same meat, the same buns that Harley cooked with. But there was something that felt better about it.

Maybell hadn't noticed any of that. Otis, a steady customer, waved her over as she passed by. Otis drove a soda route between Hadley and a distribution center outside Prescott. He came to the diner at least once a week.

"Say, Maybell, what'd ya do, change the grease?"

"Tell you what, Otis, I'll change the grease in the deep fry if you change the grease in your hair."

Otis shook his head and chuckled as Maybell walked on. She cleared a table and went behind the counter to dump the dishes in the bin. She had the change from that table and dropped it in the tip jar. That's when she first noticed something was different. Dolene was nearby, consolidating ketchup.

"Hey, Dolene, you been getting more tips today?"

Dolene hadn't thought about it, but now realized: "You know? Yeah."

"I just had Otis complimenting the food. That man would eat a dirt sandwich if it had enough ketchup."

Maybell looked over at Bill. He was less busy now, but every bit as engrossed. Bill was amazed at how all food changed when it hit the grill. How the patty started sizzling and the fat started melting. How cheese softened and oozed. How bacon crisped and potatoes crusted. But what really got him were the eggs. The way the cool, hard shell cracked. The liquid stillborn life inside. How quickly that liquid turned solid on the grill. "Eggs are change," he would later say, as if that was the most profound philosophical statement. As if that said it all.

An old guy lumbered up to the counter to pay. Dolene went to the register, and Maybell decided to have a talk with her cook.

Bill was checking the toastiness of a grilled cheese and bacon. He served it up on a plate, added French fries, slaw, and a pickle. Then he then laid it on the metal counter near the grill for Maybell. She didn't need to look it over to know it was right. But she didn't pick it up right away.

"You know something I just realized, I don't know your name."

Bill turned a burger and placed a slice of cheese on top. He looked a little uncomfortable.

After a pause she went on. "I guess what I'm doing is asking your name."

I suppose it would be giving too much away, but I still feel I have to tell you that up until this moment, Bill's name was not Bill. In fact, Bill didn't have a name at all. Why he didn't is a can of worms that I'm not ready to open just yet.

Over at the register, Dolene had just broken a twenty, and to her stunned surprise the old guy, Bill, forked over five dollars of that for a tip.

"That burger deluxe was fine," he said. Dolene was too busy staring at the five to notice the man's eyes. They looked right at her, calm and steady.

"Bill!" she exclaimed with surprise. "Thank you!"

At the grill, Bill heard that. He answered Maybell simply, "Bill."

"Okay. What's your last name?"

Bill didn't have a second answer, so he just went with the first.

"Bill."

"Bill Bill. That's your name?" Maybell looked at him. If he wanted to lie about his name, that was fine. Not everybody cared for you to know their business. Did it really matter? This guy could cook.

"Bill, I wanna offer you a job. I pay twelve an hour, no tips, no benefits, no bullshit. You want it?"

This wasn't what Bill had in mind when he got off the bus. But he could feel the heat of the grill behind him. It seemed almost alive to him, almost like a being. He thought, Eggs are change.

"Sure," he said.

The house was Maybell's, but my room belonged entirely to me. The walls were a dark gray because to my mind nothing under that roof deserved color. I didn't put up any posters for the same reason I never wore clothes with anyone's name or labels. There was no way I would let another person tell me who I was or how to think. Girls in my school spent money they didn't have on designer this and that, anything that would announce to the world that they belonged in it. I went out of my way to show I didn't. My misshapen sweatshirts, black tees and black pants came from Goodwill, often the men's side. Most of the money I had was set aside to fund my eventual escape from Hadley.

There was a lock on my door that meant, aside from sharing walls with Maybell's house, my room was completely separate, like a foreign country with its own sovereign laws. One law, really. Maybell was not allowed in.

I was on my bed, doing homework, when I heard her come home after work. She was yammering away, which meant she had a guest. I could hear her introducing Bill to Sonny Boy. Then her heavy footsteps clomped up to my door.

"Belutha! You were supposed to pick up Clover."

I shouted at the door. "I told you I had lab after school!"

"I don't remember you telling me."

"Try not getting drunk. You'll remember more."

"I'm a one-woman show here, Belutha. How about a little cooperation?"

Times like that I wished my door opened out instead of in. It would have shoved Maybell into the other wall. I unlocked the door and pulled it hard.

"My life ain't about cleaning up after your sexual blunders!"

That's when I caught sight of Bill. He was in the living room, and from the way he was looking all around, you would have thought this was his first time inside any house. He stepped up to inspect the pictures on the walls, like they were paintings hanging in a museum.

In truth, Bill didn't make much of a first impression.

I turned to Maybell. "Who the hell is this?"

Maybell played hostess. "Belutha, this is Bill. Bill, this is my daughter, Belutha. Born Caesarean sixteen years ago. I've been in pain ever since."

That was one of her favorite lines. Doctors had to cut her open to get me out of her uterus. I find that hard to believe. I would have paid to get out of there.

"Bill's my new cook," Maybell continued.

He gave me a look as if I was one of the exhibits at the museum and then turned away to see more. He caught sight of the video game Sonny Boy was playing and stepped over to see.

"Seriously, Maybell?" I said. "You're so desperate to get laid you gotta hire 'em?"

Maybell shook her head. "Bill? Gimme *some* credit." Then, to Bill: "That's not a slight on you personally." She stepped up to the TV to make an announcement. "Bill's stayin' for a few days. He's gonna bunk in with Sonny Boy."

Sonny Boy lifted his head up from the game. "That's not fair! What about the garage?"

"Is that how you welcome a guest to your home?" Maybell scolded, like she was actually a mother imparting values of some kind. "I'm gonna make us some dinner."

By making dinner, Maybell meant putting frozen food into the microwave and then onto a plate. Working all day in food service, it's pretty understandable she wanted little to do with it when she got home.

"Not for me," I said. "I don't eat that chemical-infested, cancer-causing crap." I had half a cucumber and some homemade hummus in the fridge.

"Fine," Maybell said. "More for the rest of us."

I wasn't just staring at Bill over dinner. I was staring hard, with an aim to intimidate. I think he misunderstood because he looked down at the way he was holding his fork, as if he might be doing it wrong.

Truth is, I was the one intimidated. Maybell's men usually visited for no more than a few hours, arriving after midnight and disappearing before the sun. She had no interest in sharing her bed for more than sex. And a fair portion of the guys who came around had wives to get back to. So a strange man sitting down to dinner with us was a very uncomfortable first.

Sonny Boy was utterly uninvolved, as always. If Bill was wearing a turban and shoulder strapped grenade-launcher, I don't think Sonny Boy would have looked up. It wasn't Sonny Boy I was worried about, or even me. With Bill sitting three feet from Clover, I realized like never before how vulnerable an eight-month-old can be. I felt a helplessness like I never experienced before. How easy it would be for a stranger to destroy my world.

I was equally amazed by how unbothered Maybell seemed.

"What do you know about this guy?" I asked her, pointing my fork at Bill.

"He can cook," she said. "What else do you need to know?"

"He could be a serial killer."

"Belutha, would you please not second-guess everything decision I make?"

"I don't second-guess you, Maybell. I first-guess you. You don't even get a second guess!"

Maybell put down her fork. "Bill, are you a serial killer?"

Bill looked thoughtful, as if he wasn't quite sure of the answer.

I decided I'd be sleeping with my rifle.

I walked into Sonny Boy's room. Bill's cot was made up, but Bill was nowhere around.

"Where's the serial killer?" I asked.

"He's not really a killer." It was a question. Sonny Boy was playing Temple Run on his phone.

"Probably not, I guess. All I know is Maybell brought him here, so you gotta figure something's not right."

Sonny Boy couldn't argue with that. "I think he went out back."

"What for?"

Sonny Boy shrugged. I thought it must be comforting to have no curiosity.

I went out the back door and stood a moment to give my eyes a chance to adjust. Then I saw him. He was about a hundred feet from the house, facing away. His head was angled up. He was looking at the stars. We had no houses in back of us, just desert, so there was no ambient light to diffuse the night sky. It still amazes me that, given all of Maybell's disastrous life choices, she got this one, an isolated house, just right.

I walked over, purposely making noise. I didn't think startling a potential killer was a good idea. Every step felt more precarious. I went through a catalog of all the possible ways he could turn and kill me, at least five or six scenarios in those few seconds. It seemed stupid to not have brought my rifle. I could throw a punch almost as well as a guy, but it's just not the same as a weapon.

I kept myself about five feet back in case I had to run. I'm sure he heard me, but he didn't look away from the sky.

"I got eyes in the back of my head," I said after a moment. "Anything happens tonight, I'll know."

Nothing. It was possible he didn't hear me. Or maybe he was getting ready to turn and attack me with a kitchen knife. I pictured him wearing a clown face.

"You so much as breathe on Sonny Boy, you'll be staring at the business end of a loaded rifle." It wasn't hard to sound menacing. I meant it.

He finally craned his neck to look at me. He had a smile. He didn't look threatening or threatened. I found that disconcerting. Bill's smile seemed genuine, even innocent. His eyes looked at me as if to say, "Aren't those stars amazing?" Then he turned to look up again.

I went back in the house without saying a word. "Okay," I thought. "You get round one."

Bill told me later that he didn't dream that first night.

It had been a long day that brought him to Hadley, to working the grill at Maybell's Diner, and finally to the cot in Sonny Boy's room. The exhaustion he felt when he lay down was complete and consuming.

While his body was sleeping on the cot, Bill said he found himself floating. He rose above the desert, over the town of Hadley, and higher still. Soon the lights below him seemed distant, like small constellations. He thought he could just float away and wondered if he should.

He wasn't sure exactly how he noticed it, but he became aware of something behind him. It was like the lightest weight pulling on him. He turned and saw a very thin, glowing string that connected him to the house in Hadley where his body lay.

Bill realized he was tethered to that body and that, no matter where he went, the glowing string would lead him back.

He followed that string down, closer and closer to the earth, all the way to the outside of Maybell's house. He barely took notice of a car parked on the street there. It was an old, beat-up Camaro, red with a two gray panels. Someone was inside, sleeping.

Bill kept following the thin string to where his body lay asleep on the cot in Sonny Boy's room. He watched it breathing in and out, resting up for a new day.

"A baby is born to parents who believe in this world. To a planet of people who believe in this world. To an entire history of belief in this world.

"What chance does the baby have, except to believe in this world?"

            —*Bill Bill, Interview at Maybell's Diner*

The guys at Maybell's diner weren't sure what to make of Bill. They were used to Harley. And though they didn't like his cooking, they liked him, or at least they didn't dislike him. Harley was a known quantity.

But now here was Bill, focused on the grill like nothing else mattered, so completely intent on making each egg just right, that he never even looked up. It was as if the guys had snuck into a movie about a grill cook, and the character in the movie couldn't see them.

The regulars exchanged looks. There was Radd, who I told you about before. And there were two friends of his, Wade and Oswaldo. I called them the Three Unwise Men because they spent so much time at Maybell's. The Unwise Men didn't like change. It meant they had to apply some attention to what was otherwise the dead and deadening routine they counted on.

I have a theory about men. Their problem isn't that they're stupid. I mean, they are stupid, there's no denying that. But, to be fair, women are pretty stupid too. That's just the burden of who we are, which wouldn't be so bad if we didn't have to be around each other all the time.

The problem with men isn't their natural stupidity. It's the added stupidity they voluntarily impose on themselves to get along with other men. It starts when they're boys. I know, I've seen it happen. They believe they need to act dumb in order to get along with other boys. Through their lives, they learn to cut off their own intelligence, the way a doctor cuts off a baby's foreskin. And like foreskin, that intelligence doesn't grow back. I don't know why. It's not like these men have literally snipped a physical thing. Maybe it's habit, or years of disuse, but after enough time acting dumb in order to get along with others, they stay dumb. And that pretty much accounts, in large part, for this crazy world we live in.

Of the Three Unwise Men, it was Radd who had some knowledge of this new cook. So he waited until Bill had the grill mostly cleared and then spoke up.

"Hey, howya doin'?"

Bill turned to the counter behind him, as if surprised to find himself in a diner.

Radd went on: "Yesterday, remember? Scrambled with home fries?" Radd offered his hand. "Radd."

Bill tilted his head a bit. He had heard about this; shaking hands, putting one's most valuable body part into an embrace with another. It was an experience he had hoped to have. He reached his hand out and embraced Radd's. He was surprised when Radd seemed to close his hand around his, as if he had no intention of giving it back. He could feel the warmth of Radd's hand and found the sensation comforting, though he didn't know why. There were so many impressions all at once: the scaly calluses on Radd's fingers, the subtle feel of Radd's heartbeat. But more than anything, Bill could feel Radd's good intent radiating from him like his pulse. Bill had not known so much joy could be found from one being touching another.

Radd looked at him searchingly and Bill realized why. Radd wanted to hear his name. "Bill," Bill finally said.

Maybell swung by to pick up some meals. "Boys, let the man work." She stacked four plates on one arm and went off.

Just outside the diner, Rose was walking up faster than usual. She had seen through the window that booth 4 was unoccupied. There were times Rose would drive by the diner slowly, to scope out the booth situation. If they were all full, she'd drive on. Sometimes she'd run an errand, but more often than not she'd park just off Main Street and read her book. She didn't mind the wait, because it wasn't hunger that brought her to Maybell's. She liked being near people, without necessarily interacting with them. It made her feel like she was part of something. She'd been living alone so long that any human contact, even in passing, fulfilled a basic social longing. But that longing went only so far. Sitting at a regular table, right next to others, left her feeling open to scrutiny and judgment. A booth was as much proximity as Rose could handle.

Booth 4 happened to be her favorite and when she got inside she planted her purse atop it like an American flag on the moon.

That was around the time I came to the diner with Clover. I found his bubble walker behind the counter and snapped him into the harness so his tiny feet barely touched the floor.

As I started for the door, Maybell called to me: "Belutha, you want a bite before school?"

The idea of putting anything in my body that had been touched by Maybell, either directly or through association, was anathema to me. "I despise diner food and all it stands for," I called behind me. Sometimes you had to draw a line.

Maybell stuck her tongue out at my back.

"I saw that," I said without looking back. I went out the door.

Dolene passed by Maybell with a load of dirty dishes. "She's a bundle'a sunshine, your daughter."

"Light'a my life," Maybell said flatly.

Outside, I saw a guy drinking beer on the tailgate of his pickup. It was Harley. He faced the diner, the truck faced away. I passed by without even slowing down, figuring that was the best way to show my disapproval. "A little early for beer, isn't it Harley?"

He had a snooty tone to his voice, like a boy accused of cheating. "I don't believe I offered you any."

As I turned to walk up the road, a light blue Camry pulled in to Maybell's. The driver was Rute Garlin. In his late forties, Rute kept his shirt tucked in to help manage a barrel of fat he carried everywhere. He wore a tie and short sleeves, which was standard dress for the water reclamation plant where he worked.

Today he was taking the morning off to bring his mom to the doctor. That was already an annoyance. It became worse when she insisted on coming to Maybell's first. Mrs. Garlin had lost some motor skills and her ability to speak following a stroke last fall. Because she had to leave the house to see the doctor anyway, she wanted to get breakfast at the diner beforehand. It would be the first time since the stroke, and she was aching to feel normal again.

Rute scooted around to the passenger door to help her out of the car. With his arm around her, he walked her up to the diner, the slowness of her pace seeming to pain his every step. He just wanted this morning over with.

Bill was facing away from the door when they entered. He stopped what he was doing and stood motionless. Radd saw that and thought it odd. None of the other Unwise Men noticed.

Dolene walked up to the grill.

"Bill? Bill?"

He seemed confused when he looked at her.

"Got two over hard and a short stack, extra thin."

Dolene put the order on the spindle. When she walked away, Bill turned and looked around until he spotted Rute and Mrs. Garlin. Radd had no idea what was going through Bill's mind, but it was the first time all day he saw Bill distracted.

Rute noticed several tables were free, but he didn't want his mom to get too comfortable, so he led her to the counter. Getting her seated took some doing and she kept her gaze forward, feeling others looking at her. She hated having her frailty on display.

Maybell swung by with a pot of coffee and poured some for both. "Morning, Rute. Mrs. Garlin. How's she feeling?"

Sometimes the most hurtful things we say are the things we say by accident. Like asking Rute about Mrs. Garlin, as if she wasn't right there.

"She's aw-right," Rute answered. "I'll take an egg sandwich. Mama, whatta you want?"

Mrs. Garlin would love to have answered that. But it would probably take her a good deal of time and she knew her son's impatience. He would never wait that long. Asking was his way of highlighting her weakness.

She could feel the right side of her face, like a dead mass she tried to move, but couldn't.

"Now you don't wanna see the doc on an empty stomach, do you? C'mon, Mama." She knew what Rute was up to. This was her punishment for dragging him there.

Maybell could see the cost on Mrs. Garlin. "Look, Rute, why don't I just put in an order for scrambled eggs, something easy to get down. . . ."

"Dammit, Maybell," Rute snapped. "No!"

People nearby started to turn. This was exactly the kind of attention Mrs. Garlin didn't want.

"She has to learn to talk on her own," Rute went on. "Doc said it wasn't a full-on stroke."

Mrs. Garlin felt people's eyes on her. She was tempted to turn and see. She could have moved her head that much. But she stared straight ahead and used every bit of her will not to cry.

"Now Mama, you want food, you gotta say so, or you're just gonna sit there and watch me eat."

Mrs. Garlin looked at Maybell with desperate eyes.

"Okay," Maybell said. "I'm just gonna bring her some toast and tea. . . ."

Before Rute could stop her, Bill stepped over with a plate of food. To be more specific, it was two poached eggs on dry white toast, with two half-slices of slightly melted American cheese, a thin slice of ham grilled lightly on top and, instead of home fries, a garnish of melon.

Bill set the plate before Mrs. Garlin. She moved her eyes down to see, as her head wasn't quite up to cooperating. She saw the contents and despite being partly paralyzed, her expression registered surprise. She looked back up at Bill, who smiled at her in a way that made her feel like she knew him and that he knew her.

Her eyes said to him, "Thank you" and his smile said to her "You're welcome."

Bill went back to the grill.

"What the hell?" Rute whined. "What'd I tell you, Maybell? She has to speak for herself!"

"I didn't put in that order. . . ."

"Oh, no? That's her damn favorite."

With annoyance, Rute saw his mom using her one good hand to lift a trembling bite to her mouth. He looked at Maybell accusingly. "If you didn't, who did?"

Maybell looked at Mrs. Garlin. "Enjoy your meal, honey."

Ignoring Rute, Maybell walked over to Bill at the grill. He was busy with the next three orders.

"Bill," Maybell asked, "How did you know what Mrs. Garlin wanted? Did Dolene tell you?"

Bill turned to her from the grill for a quick moment and shook his head. He was starting to worry he had done something wrong.

"Then how did you get her order? Did she pass you a note?"

Bill shook his head again and turned back to the grill.

"Well, someone must have told you. . . ."

Bill had hoped that by not looking at Maybell she would soon not be there. I could have told him that never works. He finally turned back and admitted: "I just . . ." There was a pause until he figured out the right words. "Could tell."

Bill had the look of a dog that had just chewed a pillow and expected to get punished.

"You just could tell?" she said disbelievingly.

Bill nodded. Maybell thought about that one. Well, if Bill was going to lie to her, then at the very least she was going to prove him a liar. She looked around until she spotted an older couple that had just sat down at table 3. They were looking at menus.

Maybell grimaced. "All right, what about that those two people. What do they want?"

Bill looked over at the couple. He seemed pensive, like he was deciding which shoes to wear. Then he turned back to Maybell. "She wants hotcakes with margarine on the side. Hot chocolate. He wants scrambled eggs with a side of bacon. No toast. Coffee."

Bill said that with complete surety and then turned back to the grill as though the matter was closed. At least that's what he hoped.

Maybell saw Dolene heading toward that table and waved her off. "I got this, hon." Maybell had seen this couple many times over the years. She figured they lived on the other side of Gaylordville.

"Hi folks," she said, taking out her pad. "What'll it be?"

The woman looked up from the menu and decided: "I'll have a hot chocolate. And hotcakes. No butter, but if you have margarine, I'll take that. Just a bit, in fact I'll have it on the side."

Maybell stopped writing. She felt like she had a rock in her chest.

The man spoke up. "I'll get some oatmeal and coffee."

Maybell wasn't aware she was holding her breath until she let it out.

The woman added, "Honey, you been good all week. You want eggs?"

The man turned to Maybell. "Scratch that, I'll get two eggs, scrambled. Side of bacon. Don't need any toast."

Maybell just stood there a moment. The couple looked at each other. Then Maybell pocketed her pad and pen, turned and walked away.

She walked right into the kitchen and then out the back door.

Back at the table the man turned to his wife. "They really don't like you changing your order here."

Maybell didn't know how long she had been pacing out back. At some point when she looked at the diner, she was struck by a memory from seventeen years before. It was the first time that she had ever seen the diner from the back. It was up for sale then, and she had come to take a look.

She was five months pregnant with me and desperately didn't want to be. Before my biological father's sperm had forced itself upon an egg inside her womb, Maybell felt like the whole world opened up before her like a flower. Now, with me growing bigger inside her each day, the world seemed to be closing in like a Venus flytrap.

She figured as long as she was going to be stuck in Hadley with a baby around her neck, she was going to lay down a stake. Her father had recently died and, to her surprise, left her some decision-making money.

So there she went, to the Hadley Diner, which had been sitting vacant since the owner passed a year before.

And there she was now, for the first time after all those years, standing in that exact spot where she stood when she considered buying the place.

The back door opened. Dolene poked her head out from the kitchen. "May, honey, you okay?'

Maybell thought the building looked foreign to her now, like something she didn't understand. Dolene was waiting for an answer. Maybell didn't have one.

Rodney Haas was on the prowl. He was my age, shorter than average but blessed with a trim body that would never have much fat. I couldn't say the same for the space between his ears. Like most guys in high school, his obsession was sex. Whatever spare brainpower he had beyond that was trapped and inert, as if stuck in bubble wrap.

I was at my locker after the last class ended. I didn't know it at that moment, but Rodney was tracking my movements. He kept himself on the other side of a gaggle of girls so I wouldn't see him. It was unusual for anyone there to pay attention to me.

In school, and I guess in life, there are two kinds of people. Those who belong with other people. And those who don't. Even when I was young, I was more inclined to the second category. There wasn't a lot of belonging I wanted to do. But it was still nice to have the option if I wanted.

The matter was settled for me in eighth grade.

It started with Dot Morales and her stroke of genius. Dot and I had been in each others' orbits since around kindergarten. In all that time we probably spoke twice. She was deep in the second category and didn't talk much to anyone.

On the day in question, Dot's mom handed her thirty-four dollars for a trim and blowout at Frieda's Hair Salon. Dot's life-changing idea was to pocket the money and cut her own hair. After all, who knew better the style she wanted?

The next day in school, Dot showed up with what looked like a vivisected animal on top of her head. That was all anyone could talk about that morning. When lunch came, Dot sat alone at a table in the back of the cafeteria, hoping, I guess, to disappear into the wall. Suzie Baron, a girl with both feet firmly in category one, felt duty-bound to make sure Dot suffered the proper humiliation. She stood up across the room and treated Dot to a scorching invective which, if I'm to be honest, was pretty much what most of us had been thinking.

I didn't particularly like Dot or dislike Suzie. But it always seemed cowardly to go after someone in category two. Wasn't it already hard enough to belong with no one?

I don't remember how I came to be standing in front of Suzie, shouting in her face. I for sure don't know what I was saying. Somehow the two of us got to tussling on the floor and that's when the back of my head banged into Suzie's mouth. It was never my intention to knock out her front tooth. Suzie ran off crying, leaving a spotty trail of blood on the floor. Some teacher yanked me up by the arm and dragged me to the principal's office.

I was suspended for eight days. After that I was forced to see a county therapist once a week for the rest of the school year. Because of her job, Maybell was unable to drive me the twenty-five miles for my sessions. So the therapist drove to Hadley.

Every week she'd park in the school guest spot, in full view of the classrooms on the west side of the building. We met in the gym administration office, since it was rarely used during class. I'd hear balls bouncing and kids screaming outside the door as Melinda Carpella ("Call me Lynn") tried to get me to open up.

Open up. With twenty-seven kids right outside the door. With the whole school fixated on our sessions. They'd stand and watch "Call me Lynn" making her way down the hall, on her way to visit the resident psychopath.

Dot fared better than I did. Two days after the incident, when Suzie returned to school with her lip swollen and her eyes still red, Dot approached her in the hall and said how sorry she was for what happened. She meant it. The two of them now had a common enemy in me. Their negotiations were delicate and protracted, but by the end of the year, Dot had become part of Suzie's group. She was freed from category two.

My sessions with "Call me Lynn" were pretty uneventful. She invited me to talk about my home life or anything else that came to mind. I thought it best to avoid any subject that might get me committed to an insane asylum. But eventually I came to like "Call me Lynn." While it's true she did this work for a paycheck, I could tell her only agenda was to help me. She was the first sane person I had ever known. I never felt cured of whatever mental illness I had, but I came to cherish my time with her. I suppose she was the mother I would have wanted.

That's why, in our last session together, I cried and cried and I couldn't get myself to stop. "Call me Lynn" thought I was having separation anxiety. And it's true I hated saying good-bye to the only reasonable person in my life. But there was something else. Middle school was ending, and high school was next. I was now permanently downgraded to category two. There would be no reprieve until after graduation, maybe for the rest of my life. Belonging was no longer an option. There are prom queens and football captains and geeks and druggies. I had become the school pariah. The invisible girl.

Which is why I had no reason to expect that someone, Rodney for instance, would be watching me.

I left school alone as usual and was walking down the main road when Rodney's dilapidated Chevy pickup pulled up in front of me. He had found it rusting in some junkyard and brought it back to life like a half-eaten zombie. He had a knack for engines.

In recent months I had become Rodney's sexual obsession. I couldn't figure out why. There were girls who had not foresworn the male sex and who might—for reasons beyond me—find Rodney attractive. But somehow he zeroed in on me. If he wasn't such a pest, I might have helped him see the pointlessness, so that he could be free to pursue more fertile prey.

He jumped out of the truck and lay sideways on the hood with a hand propping up his head, as if he'd been hanging out there all day.

"Yo, Belutha, what up?"

"Rodney, do you feed on rejection?"

"I'm being persistent, which is charming, 'case you hadn't heard."

"You're bein' a pest, and charm is never gonna be an option for you."

I walked around his truck without stopping.

"What'chu got there?" He motioned to an oversized book I had checked out from the school library.

"*The World Atlas,*" I said. "I'm trying to figure out where I'm gonna live after I leave Hadley and ass-buckets like you."

Rodney jumped off the truck, but kept a respectful distance. "Belutha, when are you gonna give in to your womanly nature and have sex with me?"

"Tell you what Rodney, after I'm dead you can have fifteen minutes with my corpse."

I continued down the road without looking back. He could have followed me and made my walk shitty. I hand it to Rodney for not doing that.

As I reached Maybell's diner, something caught my eye. There were more cars than usual for this time of day. For a moment I wondered if we had gotten out of school early.

Inside, people were mostly silent. There was some whispering now and then. But you could hear the scrape of a fork on plate, it was that quiet.

Everyone had their eyes on Roy. He was a retired fireman who had bought a place with a few acres about five miles off the main road. Right now, Roy was hungry and getting impatient. His fingers were strumming the counter. Looking down at his empty coffee cup made him more annoyed. He saw Dolene passing behind him, carrying some plates of food.

"Hey, Miss, how about taking my order?"

Dolene was a terrible liar. "Uhm, sorry. . . . Not my station."

Roy was going to say something, but Dolene scooted away too fast.

The sound of clanging dishes caught his attention. Maybell pulled out a dirty bin from under the counter and handed it off to a local high school senior she hired to clean her dishes. Maybell tapped local students, paying them less than minimum under the table. Most were just happy for a reason to get out of school.

As Maybell passed Roy, he reached for her arm. "Hey, Maybell, c'mon, I'm sitting right here. I just wanna get a—"

Maybell held out her hand. "Whoa, whoa, easy Roy. I just need ya to—" Maybell looked over at the grill. Bill lifted a hot sandwich off the grill and nodded to Maybell. She nodded back.

"Sit tight, I got your lunch coming right now." Maybell went to the grill before Roy could say anything. Bill added some fried onions, a scoop of coleslaw and two quarter-pickles. He and Maybell exchanged a silent look as she took the plate and brought it to Roy.

Roy was confused. "I didn't even order yet."

"I know," she said. "Is this what you were gonna order?"

Roy looked down at the plate. He lifted one side of the grilled rye bread. Inside, two slices of nicely melted cheese surrounded a hamburger patty. Roy looked at the slaw and pickles and shook his head, like someone had just hit him. He turned to Maybell.

"What the hell? How did you know?"

Roy was surprised by the burst of cheers and clapping around him. They all had been waiting silently for this moment, as they had for a similar moments that had been happening over the last two hours. Lunch stragglers like Roy had their orders mind-read. Those that did and those that watched were sticking around to see it happen again.

Coming to this party late, I had no idea what was going on. I unbuckled Clover from the bubble walker and put him in the baby carrier that I left under the counter. When I stood back up with Clover at my belly facing the world, the Unwise Men were shaking Bill's hand and patting him on the back. I saw Dolene to my left, looking at Bill with a strange expression, a mix of fear and desire. The customers were smiling and talking to each other like I've never seen people do in that town, even after church.

Maybell suddenly came to me and put her unwelcome hands on each side of my face.

"Did you see that?" she roared. "That's been going on all day."

"What?" I said, pulling my face out of reach.

"Bill! Don't ask me how, but he knows what people want before they order!"

Maybell went to stand by Bill's side, as if to proclaim he was her discovery and no one else was welcome to him.

Bill stood at the center of all this. He seemed confused, but pleased. People were smiling at him. I could see he wasn't quite sure why, but he was glad for it. There was a hint of modesty, a little bit of joy. But as he reached to shake the hands offered to him, I could see there was something else that no one there seemed to notice. Along with the gladness, Bill was afraid.

It was 4:46 a.m. in Phoenix Memorial Hospital. There was usually a lull around this time. An orderly was napping behind a curtain in the ER. Two nurses were making coffee at their station. Doctor Gording was filling out paperwork on a fatality brought in at 3:43 a.m. It was a young man with a drug overdose. He was semi-comatose when he got there and never regained consciousness. The time of death was 4:32 a.m. Doctor Gording ordered the body left in a darkened recovery room until six a.m., when the morgue downstairs would open.

Bill saw all that. The napping orderly. The brewing coffee. The doctor wiping his tired eyes. And he saw the body. An overwhelming number of its brain cells had been damaged from lack of oxygen. That was good, actually. Bill didn't want issues with the previous occupant's memory.

The body was young. And, aside from the drug use, it was in good shape.

Bill says he looked at it from above for some time. He was hesitant. Even doing this, coming in for a short time, seemed really scary to him. He had no idea what to expect. But then that was the whole point: to experience something he never had before. He had been wanting to do this for a long time. This is what he kept telling himself over and over. And he knew his window was closing fast. In a few more minutes, too many brain cells would be dead.

Bill started to think himself forward, and so he moved forward. He found himself rushing all at once to that face, the skin, the marrow, the billions and trillions of cells that now danced loudly around him. He said everything went gray and strange. He couldn't see, but he could sense a connection to something. He described it as a network, as a bunch of networks actually, all interconnected. It was like a conglomeration that was more intricate than anything he had known. The systems were silent at first, but slowly they began making noise. Just by Bill being there, it was like a switch had been turned on. The noise was building. Bill was terrified. He had never felt anything as powerful or out of control.

He was about to get out of there, when this wave hit him with a crash. He felt something physical. Later, he realized it was nausea. That was his first sensation as a human. Welcome to my world, Bill.

He thought: "Leave!" But this thing already had a momentum. There was a convulsion. An overwhelming tidal wave. All the systems started to come alive at once, causing a massive upheaval. The body of the man jolted with a huge spasm. Its eyes opened suddenly, and it drew a breath.

Bill was here.

It took a while for Bill to figure out limbs and movement. Just getting that body to sit up was a monster effort. Through its eyes he saw a pile of clothes in a plastic bag nearby and figured they were for the body. He said getting dressed was the hardest thing he had ever done. But he didn't have much time. They'd come for him soon.

The hospital video would later show Bill stepping out into the hallway at 5:42 a.m. He looked wobbly, but otherwise didn't stand out. He passed the orderly who had been napping before and had just woken up. Bill tipped his head down, so as not to be noticed. He walked by the admitting station to his left.

To his right, the waiting room was nearly empty. An older woman with asthma was next to go in. In the back of the room, there were two people; a young man and a woman. Like Bill, they looked like life had dealt them shit hands. Or maybe they had chosen those hands. The young woman was sobbing into the young man's shoulder. Her name was Katie. The young man, Cyril, was facing the room when something drew his eye. He was stunned. He had just seen Bill.

Bill kept walking. There was a security guard up ahead by the door. Bill wondered if he would be stopped. The thought turned into a fear, and the fear expressed itself in his body through a faster heart rate. Bill thought: increased blood flow enables fight or flight. Even now, with its second occupant, this body was built to survive. Bill marveled at it.

When he made it out the door he felt a wave of relief. His heart slowed. The body had adjusted to its changing circumstances that quickly.

Bill had made it to the road when he had his first real look at the world through a pair of eyes. He was stunned at the dramatic difference between being inside a building and outside. The sky was gray, but already getting lighter. Above the buildings there was a partial view of the horizon. A slight bit of orange was beginning to show.

The sight was so furiously full and overwhelming, he literally could not move his body. Until this moment he thought the sense of sight was just a poor excuse for perceiving the world, channeling all that is around into a narrow spectrum of light and shape. But faced with it now for the first time, he felt shattered. It seemed so loud and vibrant. And the thing that surprised him most of all was that it appeared endless. This finite world seemed infinite.

He didn't notice the bus until it stopped right in front of him. Bill had been standing these few minutes at a bus stop. The driver waited for Bill to get on, and when Bill didn't move, the driver operated the hydraulics, causing the bus to lower down. Over the years, he had picked up a lot of very shaky people outside this hospital. Often he let them ride free.

The driver said to Bill, "You coming?"

Bill thought, Why not?

He got onto the bus. The driver raised the bus and took off for points west: last stop Hadley.

Standing in the hospital doorway, Cyril saw all this. He was still reeling in shock. He thought of going back inside to tell Katie. And he knew for dead certain she'd be furious if he just left her there without a word. But even that was better, he realized, than her knowing what he saw. Luckily, the bus always traveled the same route. It wouldn't be hard to catch up to it. He walked quickly across the street and got into his beat up old red Camaro with its two panels painted in a streaky gray color.

"People think of life on earth as being what's normal. They believe this is where life exists. They think that, if there is the possibility of life elsewhere, it would be on the same terms as here. In other words, it would be on a planet.

"But the fact is, any kind of planetary life is pretty unnatural.

"It's just that you've gotten used to it."

—Bill Bill, *Interview at Maybell's Diner*

Bill sat at the middle tier of the bleachers, looking to his left and right and all around, as if he had no idea the whole reason for being there was to look straight ahead at a ballgame.

The Hadley Roadrunners were playing the Gaylordville Saints. I don't know why they bothered naming their teams, since no one wore uniforms. My guess is it made them all feel a little more legitimate and self-important. It also helped when they told their wives they wouldn't be around for three hours. It sounded better than "I'm drinking beer with the boys," which was pretty much the point.

I sat at the top of the bleachers, away from everyone. Sometimes I'd come to these games to do my homework. When my focus started to drift, I'd look over at the drunken guys trying to relive the glory days of their youth. That always motivated me to study harder.

That day, though, I was there to check out Bill. After that first night he had become an enigma to me, which was unusual since most guys tended to be overly simple. I was no longer of the mind that he posed a threat. I just wanted to figure him out.

There was a respectable crowd in the bleachers, mostly friends and wives, about thirty in all. Maybell and Marguerite sat up front, close to first base, talking so much I wondered, as I always did, how it was they never ran out of things to say. Sonny Boy sat watching Clover two rows behind them. That, for Sonny Boy, meant playing a game on his phone and having no idea if Clover was alive, breathing, or existed on the planet.

Marguerite was on her third beer. "How do you think he does it?"

Maybell shook her head. "Hell if I know. Not a bad quality, though, for a grill cook."

"How's his cooking?"

"Better'n mine."

"My border collie can cook better'n you."

Maybell laughed and pulled on her beer. "Honey, you remember that cousin of yours, the one you once fixed me up with?"

"Harold?"

"Yeah. What became of him?"

"You looking for a date?"

"Oh, Lord, no. He was more awkward than a hernia. I just was wondering. . . . Didn't you say he used to blog for some big magazine?"

"Yeah, he's freelance. Mostly trash stuff. Tabloids and whatnot."

Maybell was trying to downplay her interest. "Yeah, that's right. So ya think he might want to do a story on Bill?"

"Will it get him laid?"

"It might." Maybell took a swig. "Not by me, though."

The two of them laughed.

I looked over at Bill. He was oblivious to the plans Maybell was making for him. Oblivious to the game. A starling flew over the field and Bill turned to see. Then he noticed an airplane flying overhead. It was barely a speck, passing high in the sky over country that didn't matter to anyone on board. Bill was riveted.

I went down to sit next to him.

"Hey," I said, louder than necessary. I wanted to make him uncomfortable.

He looked at me and didn't say a word. Then he looked back up at the airplane. He seemed disappointed as it flew out of view. Then, to my surprise, he looked at me again, right at me this time. Now I was uncomfortable.

"Can I ask you a question?" He had something on his mind.

"Sure," I said.

"What do you see up there?"

I didn't have to look up to tell him. "The sky."

"What color it is?"

"Blue, mostly."

"But it's not really blue—right?"

I saw what he was getting at.

"No, it just looks blue."

He looked at me and nodded, like he and I just shared an important secret. Then he looked up again and that was that. I was totally forgotten.

At home plate, a handsome, compact guy, maybe thirty-five, was getting ready to hit a homer. You could see it the way he held his bat. He was going to wake everyone up and set the game on fire. But limited talent dashed his plans, as it probably had most of the rest of his dreams in life. He hit a short high pop right to Otis in deep shortstop and for all of Wayne's frantic running, he was out before he reached first base.

Maybell was grabbing some barbecued chips when she noticed him.

"Wayne?"

Marguerite was checking her phone. Maybell gave her shoulder a push.

"Isn't that Wayne? I didn't know he was playing for Gaylordville."

Marguerite shrugged.

Maybell called to Wayne who trotted back from first base with the faintest limp that he tried to hide. "Wayne! Hey, Wayne, it's me!"

Whatever pain he felt in his leg paled compared to the pain of seeing my mom. "Oh, hey, Maybell." He kept walking, hoping a wave would suffice to shut her up.

"Aren't ya gonna say hi, Wayne." Her words were casual, but her tone was unmistakable. She was flirting.

Reluctantly, Wayne stopped walking. "Yeah. Hey." Marguerite looked up and Wayne gave her the faintest nod.

Maybell kept flirting. "How come you never come to town? Don't ya like me anymore, Wayne?"

Wayne looked at anything that wasn't Maybell. "I can't talk right now," he said. "I'm playin'."

"So'm I, Wayne. I'm playin'. You wanna play with me?" In the off-chance Wayne hadn't seen her cleavage, Maybell brushed it with her finger.

Wayne was struck dumb, like a computer going into lock-screen.

Maybell relented. "Oh, c'mon, Wayne, I'm just kiddin'. Lighten up. Look who's here. It's your son. Sonny Boy." Maybell pointed to where Sonny Boy sat with Clover. "You can finally meet him. C'mon, Wayne, he ain't gonna bite."

Wayne looked sick. He leaned a bit closer to Maybell. "I told you when—that I wasn't ready to be a father. I did tell you, May. I should get back. . . ."

When Wayne strode back to his team, his limp was gone.

Maybell frowned. "Little chicken shit," she muttered.

She and Marguerite watched him disappear behind his teammates.

"He probably just feels a little bad," Marguerite said. "You don't still, you know, have a thing for. . . ."

"Wayne? Nah." Maybell thought about it. "He's too undamaged." She gave a laugh that she wasn't fully feeling. Some mistakes never go away. That's the problem with babies. We just grow up and keep getting bigger, as if to remind people of their worst failures.

Bill seemed almost excited when he announced he had to pee. The game was over and we were walking back to Maybell's truck. He went off to the men's restroom, which was just a cinderblock enclosure with a metal urinal and toilet.

None of us noticed the old red Camaro parked across the lot, or the gaunt guy who stepped out now and walked quickly to the men's room.

Bill was at the urinal when Cyril walked in. Cyril kept his left hand down by his leg. He was holding a Bowie knife just out of sight.

"Don't turn around," Cyril ordered.

For you future robbers, you should know that when you're behind someone and order "Don't turn around," that's the fastest way to get them to turn around. You want to say something like "Freeze!"or better yet, just sneak up and put a bag over their heads. Cyril didn't know that of course. Bill turned and looked right at him. But it didn't seem to matter.

"I'll be done in a minute," Bill said, facing forward again.

Cyril was momentarily at a loss. "You mind telling me what the hell you're doing here?"

Bill looked down. "My kidneys filter waste from my blood. That waste is called urine. It leaves my body through my penis."

Cyril had no idea what to make of that. He shook it off. "So you just got up and walked out of that hospital like nothing happened?"

But Bill wasn't listening. He finished and zipped up his fly. He stepped up to Cyril who backed up quickly, his grip tightening on the Bowie knife.

"You know the penis is the only organ in the body that serves two completely different functions. Do you know what they are?"

"Yeah, I know what the fucking penis does! Look, Katie's my girl now. She says she loves me. She says I'm dependable and shit. What the hell are you? You just got on a bus and went away."

Bill looked at Cyril simply. "I don't know anyone named Katie."

Bill turned to wash his hands.

"Yeah. Awright. You just keep it that way. Or I'll take you out and it'll be for real this time. You hear me?!"

When Bill turned to him, Cyril flinched, dropping his knife. It clanged on the concrete floor.

"I do," Bill said agreeably.

Cyril thought about going for the knife, but he also wanted to get out of there. He figured the Bowie knife was a fair trade for Katie. He turned and left.

The mighty man rode hard at night while others slept, for he was mighty and others were not. His Harley took him across state lines at a hundred plus miles per, as he feared not speed, nor cop, nor oncoming vehicle. The mighty man's mighty engine roared beneath him, like a super volcano between his legs, reined in by the power of his loins. Those same loins drove him through the night, across the country, to the trailer-and-a-half home in Hadley, Arizona.

There, he cut his engine and calmly stroked his Harley, like a cowboy patting his horse. And though it was the middle of the night, he went up to that home and knocked hard on the door. He and his loins would not be denied. For he was a mighty man.

And the earth's biggest asshole.

Maybell heard the knocking and lifted her head. It was 2:49 am. "Sonofabitch," she muttered, throwing on her robe.

She opened the door and saw the mighty man, tall in her doorway, wind practically blowing through his thinning mane of black and gray hair. To the man's mind, he could have been holding a bottle of aftershave or a pack of Marlboro in some magazine ad. He believed he looked that good.

Maybell just stared.

The mighty man spoke: "'How ya doin', Oren? C'mon in, Oren. You must be tired after that long ride.'"

Without a word, Maybell punched Oren square in the mouth. I wish I could have been there in person to see it. The mighty man, my asshole father, sucker-punched by a woman.

And then just like that, Maybell put her arms around him and kissed him so hard, neither of them could breathe. Together, as one writing heap of flesh, they made their way into Maybell's bedroom.

I wouldn't think of putting you through their disgusting sex scene. The thought is repulsive to me, as I'm sure it would be for you. It was that same kind of foul event that brought me into this world. Those are two people whose genitals should never be allowed in the same state. Yet there they were, less than the sum of their parts, repeating past mistakes.

Oren had a thin, craggy face, as if years of wind beating against it on the road had chipped away at his flesh. He kept his hair long in defiance of age, a Fuck You to his slowly receding hairline. He wore leather because he knew it made him look badass, and the Harley gave him the perfect excuse. Whatever rugged, manly exterior he cultivated, he was still an immature teenager inside, the kind who celebrated his right to roam free, like a birthday party that he never wanted to end.

Biologically, it's true that a foul, self-interested part of himself swam its way up my mother's uterus and was in part responsible for my human condition. That one sperm cell was our only link. It was pleasure, not love, that brought Oren to Maybell's bed. It was utter lack of love that caused him to live a life wholly suited for himself. Even Maybell seemed like a model parent by comparison. Oren had been my first exposure to the selfish, pleasure-taking, useless nature of men.

After their revolting act of lovemaking was done, Oren sat on Maybell's bed with his back against the wall, rolling a cigarette. I don't think he liked the taste of hand-rolled. I just think he liked how rolling them made him look. Maybell was still reverberating from a satisfaction her body hungered for daily, all of her adult life.

"Lord, nobody smells like you," she said.

"You sure get my goat like no one else."

Maybell snorted. "Your goat?? Is that what I got? I thought it was your willie." Maybell fondled a part of Oren that I don't want to mention here. By now it was after four a.m. and that part had sense enough to be sleeping.

"Baby, how's our daughter doing?" Oren asked, meaning me.

Maybell let him go and rolled over. "You sure know how to kill the mood."

Oren licked the paper and tightened the cigarette, lighting it with his Zippo.

"I think she's become the patron saint of celibacy," Maybell went on.

"Good. Her age, she shouldn't be foolin' around."

"I mean *my* celibacy. She doesn't want me to have any dating life at all. Truth is, that girl is a mess."

Oren took a drag and stroked Maybell's head. "Well, sure, lookit her parents." He leaned in to kiss her. Maybell wasn't having it now.

"Why do you do this, Oren? You just come an' go. Like the flu."

"But I always come back." Oren leaned in again to kiss her. She sat up and faced away. "Oh, c'mon baby, don't be like that," he said.

Maybell stayed silent, so Oren continued. "Sure I go with other women. But none of them—par none—hold a candle to you."

Maybell turned to face him. "That's romantic, Oren! Woo me with stories of the women you fuck!" She swung at him and he blocked her hand. They both knew she could have punched him with the other if she wanted. It wasn't that kind of fight.

"I don't apologize for what I am," he said. "I'm a free bird, and this bird you cannot change."

"You know, Oren, there's a lot been going musically over the last thirty years. You should find a new song."

Oren leaned in closer. He started to sing, both really badly and with no embarrassment. It was a potent combination. "Takin' care of business. Everyday. Takin' care of business an' workin' overtime. C'mon."

Despite herself, Maybell chuckled. Oren laid his cigarette atop a near-empty beer can and put his arms around her. She wasn't fighting him this time.

I won't disgust you with what happened next.

It was the smell that woke me up, a combination of cigarettes and engine oil, road, and man. Everyone had their own unique smell and Oren's made me want to gag. I jumped up and threw on my clothes.

I found the two of them in the kitchen. Maybell was making coffee. They were both bleary from lack of sleep. Maybell didn't seem to mind. She was hooked on Oren, like a toothless junkie on meth.

"What the hell is *he* doing here?" I demanded. "You let him into my house?"

"Your house?" Oren looked at me like he wasn't sure where we had met. "I don't recall your name being on the deed."

"I don't recall a sign outside that says Deadbeat Assholes Welcome."

"That's how you talk to your father?"

I turned to Maybell. "I can't keep cleaning up after your messes! If you're so hell-bent on running your life into a brick wall, do me a favor and drop me off."

Oren's look at Maybell said, "What the hell's with her?" Maybell replied with a shrug.

I was about to march out of the kitchen when Bill entered. He had just woken up and sleepily grabbed a mug off the shelf to pour himself some coffee.

Oren looked at Maybell. "Who in the hell is this?"

I turned back to Oren. "Oh—Maybell didn't tell you? Oren, this is Bill. He's a very talented cook. He's got a lot of talent in other ways too, if you know what I mean." I raised my eyebrows a few times, in case he didn't.

Oren turned to Maybell. "You got your grill cook living with you?"

I answered before Maybell could. "Well, you know a woman gets lonely, Oren. A woman has needs."

Bill reached a hand out to Oren. "Good to meet you, Oren."

Instead of shaking his hand, Oren moved closer to Bill in a kind of nature-documentary, aggressive male way. "'Good to meet you, Oren,'" he mocked. "Well, not'sa good to meet you, Bill. Not'sa damn good at all!"

Maybell chuckled, amused by this side of Oren. She took Bill by the arm to lead him away. "I'd let you two get acquainted, but Bill's got work to do." She paused to lean toward Oren. "Don't worry, Oren. I don't do the help. I got plenty'a other options."

Maybell was glad to see Oren jealous. After she walked away, he stood at the open door, his arms pressed against each side as if to show off at least to the empty kitchen that he had muscles.

"When you're newly born, you're given a name. In your case, that name is Harold.

"Now you're defined. Your boundary stops at your skin. Everything inside your skin is Harold. Everything outside your skin is not Harold.

"Harold began with his birth and will end at his death. That means you are finite and separate from everything in the universe that isn't Harold.

"To me, that condition seems unbearably lonely."

—Bill Bill, Interview at Maybell's Diner

When Harold wrote about the encounter, he included the part where he and his cousin Marguerite met outside Maybell's Diner. He wrote that he was skeptical about some supposed mind-reading grill cook, but that he suddenly had an opening that morning and decided to go where the muse sent him.

That's what he wrote. What he didn't write about was the intense excitement he'd felt since Marguerite called and mentioned Maybell's name. Harold and Maybell had had one date about eight years before, and he had spent months afterwards beating himself up over it. He had taken her to the Fuddruckers in Gaylordville. Maybell ordered a margarita pitcher for them both, and Harold said he wasn't drinking because he was driving. He thought it would impress her. It did the opposite. She shut down to Harold, and the date was pretty much over, even as they sat through an hour of lemon chicken and penne Alfredo. She openly threw herself at the waiter while Harold just watched. If only he had shared that pitcher! He thought afterwards: better to drive into a tree than miss out on a hot woman like that.

Harold imagined this upcoming meeting as his chance to finally make up for his past mistake. He wasn't a bad looking guy. He had kept most of his hair into his mid-thirties and had an okay build. His problem was a lack of confidence, growing deeper over the years, which made his every step seem awkward.

Once inside the diner, when Marguerite went off to find Maybell, Harold noticed a couple at a table near him. They looked to be in their late fifties. Dolene had just stepped up to them with her pad.

"You folks want me to take your order, or you want it mind-read?"

The woman thought a moment and then closed her menu decisively. "You know, I'm gonna go for mind-read."

The man looked at her and they shared a nod. "Same with me. So what now? Do we concentrate, or something?"

"No," Dolene said. "Just be regular."

Dolene took their menus and went off. Harold reached into his pocket in a way that no one could see and activated the recorder app on his phone. He was beginning to wonder if maybe this thing wasn't a complete joke.

Maybell came over with Marguerite.

"May, you remember my cousin, Harold?"

Maybell held out her hand. Harold tried with all his might to force his eyes away from Maybell's breasts. There was no way around them. There were not one, but two celestial bodies and his eyes were but tiny spaceships, powerless against the force of their gravity.

Maybell pretended not to notice. "How're you doing, Harold?"

"Uhm, good. You?"

"Thanks for comin' out. So Margie told you about our cook? I bet you thought I was just tryin' to get a second date!" Maybell put her hand gently on Harold's chest just below his shoulder. It didn't hurt to keep the man hopeful. She wanted him motivated to write a good article. To say that Harold was putty in her hands was redundant. All men were putty in her hands and Maybell was the sculptress from hell.

Maybell led Harold and Marguerite to two stools at the counter. "You just relax now and let Bill figure out what you want."

Harold looked at Bill over at the grill. He hoped Bill would not be able to mind-read his hunger for Maybell.

In his article, Harold had skipped ahead to the part where Maybell laid out a plate before him. It had three pieces of French toast, made from thick white bread, with little tendrils of egg that had oozed and cooked on the grill. The proportion of powdered sugar and cinnamon was perfect in a way no one had ever done. The bacon on his plate looked exactly like the bacon in his mind. Maybell poured him a decaf per Bill's instruction and likewise laid down three half-and-halfs. Harold's stunned reaction was a combination of surprise and hunger. It was exactly what he had wanted. And it tasted even better than it looked.

After Harold was done eating, Maybell pulled Bill over to meet him.

"Bill, Harold's gonna write an article about the diner and about you. You just answer his questions, okay?"

As Harold shook hands with Bill, he found it hard to meet his eyes. It really did seem like Bill had read his mind, and Harold didn't want him poking around in there now. He kept his eyes on Maybell.

"Could we maybe find some place quiet to talk?"

"Sure." She motioned for Harold to come behind the counter. "I'll park you boys in the kitchen. It's nice an' quiet."

As Maybell led them away, she called back, "Dolene, Bill's on a break. You take orders. I'll be cookin'!"

Harold sat across from Bill at the cold metal prep table. The kitchen was both cramped and cluttered, a terrible combination. Maybell had sent the dishwasher out on a break and the pile in the sink was already scary-high.

Harold made sure his phone was recording and began.

"So, your name is Bill. . . . Bill?"

Bill nodded.

"Not William Bill or Bill Williams?"

Bill shook his head.

"How do you know what people want to eat, Bill?"

Bill shrugged.

"You don't know how?"

Bill shook his head. "Not really, no."

"Do you have other psychic abilities?"

Bill considered that. "Not that I know of."

"Do you . . . talk to dead people? Do you know which way the stock market is heading?"

Bill shook his head. "No."

Harold thought about the ninety-plus-mile drive to get there, the money in gas plus his time. He didn't know if he was going to be charged for that breakfast. If not, that would offset the expense somewhat. And though he was flustered like a teenager around Maybell, here in the kitchen he could clearly see that she had zero interest in him. This was all about getting some free press for her diner. When he studied journalism at New Mexico State, this was not what he had in mind.

Yet he wasn't ready to write off the whole morning. That French toast and bacon were still in his mind.

"Well, Bill, can you tell me anything at all? Like, where're you from?"

That was the question, looking back, that set the article in motion and sent Harold's career to a whole new level. Afterwards, he set a guideline for himself with all future interviews: always start with the basics.

"The word 'where' doesn't actually apply," Bill said. "Not everything exists in space as you understand it."

Harold just assumed Bill was kidding. "Well, what I meant to say was, where were you born?"

"I wasn't born."

Bill said that so simply and with not a spec of irony. Harold thought he just wasn't getting the joke, but no matter how hard he looked, he couldn't find it.

"Okay, I'm sorry. So you weren't—I'm a little confused. So you weren't born?"

Bill shook his head.

"Then, well, if you weren't born, how are we having this conversation?"

Harold was still trying to humor Bill in whatever joke he was trying to tell.

"This body had a previous occupant who left when the body died. He was finished with it, so I . . . I don't know what the word is. I don't think there is a word for this. I'm the new occupant."

Harold kept looking at Bill, for the punch line or for the twist or something. Bill could see he was confused and went on.

"His body was still in good shape for the most part. You can see it's doing fine."

Harold instinctively unlocked his phone to make sure it was still recording. He felt a wave of relief when he saw the red button lit. He was still lost, but thought it best to keep this conversation going. "So you were—you went and you occupied that body?"

Bill nodded.

"Where were you before that? Are you an alien?" Harold became suddenly aware there were a good number of knives nearby.

"No," Bill said simply. "This is my first time on any planet."

There was another pause. Harold stared at the unassuming expression on Bill's face. Two things became clear to him at once. First, that Bill absolutely believed what he was saying. Second, that Bill would never hurt him. Suddenly the kitchen took on a whole new light. Before, it felt like a cramped little shithole. Now it seemed fascinating and full of possibility. Harold felt heady, like he could just keep going without any fear. That was a new sensation for him.

"Well, so let me ask you, how do you like it so far? Being here, I mean."

Bill considered a moment. "More than I thought I would. People have been really nice. I like the food. Mostly, I'm surprised by the senses."

"You mean . . . like the sense of sound and sight?"

Bill nodded.

Harold placated, "Yeah, they're pretty amazing."

There was a pause. Harold knew there were journalists who had career-defining moments. He supposed this might be his. Bill wasn't just a nut. He was a nut who could read minds. Harold had experienced it. As he kept the conversation going, a portion of his brain searched for similar stories out there, and he found none.

"So what, ah, brought you here. To our world?"

Bill thought about that. It took a while before he spoke. Harold half-expected him to suddenly say, "Ha! Just kidding!"

"Well," Bill finally started. "Like most of you, I wanted to experience it. But I didn't want to be born."

"Oh, yeah? Any particular reason?"

"Well, the thing is, when you're born, memory doesn't come with you."

"Memory of what?"

Bill knew this question would probably come up at some point. He thought he'd have more time here before it did. "I don't think I'm supposed to tell you."

Harold could tell Bill was thinking about ending the interview. What did successful journalists do at such moments? They didn't let it end. Harold felt himself at a turning point, where his life could go in one of two directions. The first was back to the dull, predictable version he had always known. The Harold he had always been. The other opened a door into new possibilities he hadn't yet contemplated, even during fantasies of sex and fame. He needed to find a way to pry that door open.

"You know what I think?" Harold said. "I think you need to get this off your chest. I think this is your chance. And if you don't go for it, you'll always wonder afterwards, 'Why didn't I?'" Harold was drawing on his own experience in life in order to connect with his subject. That was one of the few lessons he remembered from college.

Bill considered that for a long moment. Harold expected him to get up and go back to his cooking.

Instead, Bill pulled up his chair. He looked at Harold and began to talk.

Eighty-three minutes later, Harold walked from the kitchen back into the diner. Pockets of sweat had run down his shirt. He didn't realize until the cooler air hit him how hot it was back there. The lighting in the diner was different now. The angle of the sun had changed. But it was more than that. The world seemed different to him. Like he could never go back to the life he had had. He both missed it and felt disdain for it.

Maybell came up to him. "You boys were at it a long time. Did ya get what you needed?"

Harold looked at her. He had thought about her so many times over the years, while lying in his bed, wracked with pain and yearning. Now she was completely neutral for him. Why was that? Maybe it was Bill's story, or his calming presence. Harold realized it didn't particularly matter. It was a relief. His desire was like a boil that had mercifully been lanced.

"Yeah," he answered. He looked around the diner. Marguerite had already left. Bill put his apron back on and returned to the grill, as though he had been on a five-minute break. As though the world hadn't changed.

Harold had no time to lose. He turned and went out to his car.

It wasn't time that Maybell was fighting. Her concern was less about growing old and more a feeling that she hadn't yet lived. It was as if her heart stopped beating when mine started, and she had to find some way to preserve her body so that when her heart started up again she could go back to living. Hence the regular trips to Frieda's.

I practically pulled the door off its hinges. Bill sat in a row of chairs along the sidewall, thumbing through a fashion magazine like an old woman waiting for a perm. I felt him look up and ignored him. I found Maybell in the back, her hair already wrapped in foil.

"Why me?!" I demanded.

"Sonny Boy can't do it."

"Why am I always your babysitter?"

"Just for the afternoon. Take my credit card from my purse. And get him some new clothes."

My jaw tightened. "Fine! But you owe me!"

I grabbed her Discover Card and stormed back to the door. I didn't even look at Bill. "Let's go!"

I heard him get up and follow me out.

I sat four rows behind Bill so we wouldn't have to talk. As it happens, I didn't have to bother. During the twenty-minute ride to Gaylordville, Bill kept his face pressed against the bus window. He seemed fascinated by the rocks and plants and all the emptiness in between. He was equally entertained by the moisture forming on the bus window from his breath.

I estimated his emotional age to be about five.

The third stop in Gaylordville was the mall entrance. There are terrible places on this earth, where children are bombed and refugees drown and the air is too polluted to breathe. This mall was the worst place in my world. The pretty lights and comfy music are only there to lull people into a compliant state so they'll spend their money. Yet they go there to relax, as if it's a trip to the beach. I suppose cattle are always the last to know they're being led to the slaughter.

My system for mall survival was simple: stay focused, go directly to what you want to buy, then head for the nearest exit. That was impossible with Bill. He stopped to look in every store, like a dog savoring each urine-soaked blade of grass.

At the top of the escalator we came upon two massage chairs, each the size of a small car. Before I could stop him, Bill deposited four quarters in one and sat down while the chair proceeded to squeeze his body like a lemon.

I sat in the dormant chair next to him to wait out those three agonizing minutes. Out of the corner of my eye I saw a security guard hold up his phone to register at a check-in station on the wall. Then he noticed us and started over. I figured he was going to boot me off the chair unless I paid for it. But that wasn't what he had in mind.

"Hi," he said. "You're Maybell's daughter—right?"

I looked up at his face. He was probably in his mid-thirties, a little chubby and with a waxy complexion that I figured came from eating mall food everyday. It was hard to remember him because all Maybell's Jerkoff Du Jours looked the same to me.

He tried to guess, "You're . . . Betty?"

"You got the B right. Let's leave it at that."

"How's your mom doing these days?"

"You mean, *who's* she doing? It's hard to keep track because she does every jerkoff in town."

Jerkoff laughed uncomfortably. "Well, tell her Andrew says hey."

"Sure, Andrew. I was hoping one of the million guys she slept with would ask me to say 'hey.'"

Andrew didn't have the bandwidth in his emotional radio to take in that kind of hostility. Or maybe he was just too locked into mall etiquette for anything that wasn't polite. He nodded and said, "Bye."

"You forgot to say, 'Have a nice day,'" I told him.

He paused. Maybe he was even about to say it. Then he realized I was mocking him. I could see the hurt land on his face. He turned and walked away.

It felt like a rifle shot went through me. Here was one of the guys who had plundered my house for sex, and yet I was the one causing pain. That's when it occurred to me for the first time that some of the men who slept with Maybell were actually hoping for more than just a joy-ride. Some, like Andrew, were probably lonely and looking to my mom of all people to find something resembling a home. I supposed that, with her maturing beauty and three kids, Maybell seemed to offer just that.

To this day, it never ceases to amaze me how deceiving looks can be.

I thought of going after Andrew to apologize, but figured that would only make things worse. Guys don't like hearing "Sorry I hurt your feelings" from a girl. As Andrew disappeared around a corner, the motor in Bill's chair came to a stop. He didn't move.

"Bill, you okay? Bill?"

He wanted to answer, but couldn't get the words to come out. He held up his hand as if to acknowledge he was still alive. If we weren't

behind enemy lines, I might have found that funny. I rose and took his
arm.

"We have to keep going."

I gave Bill a tug and he stood. He was barely able to manage one
foot in front of the other. I've never seen anyone on heroin, but I imagined that's what it would look like. At least I could get him into the
store now.

Anchor Blue was where you went for cheap, basic clothes that
passed for fashionable. I never got anything from there, but that
wasn't for lack of Maybell trying. Bill, up until then, had only the grimy
threads he wore to town and a few things of Oren's that Maybell had
kept around. At least those were unique. Now Bill was going to look
like every other guy in America.

We stood in the door and scanned the store. "Maybell's gonna pay
for whatever you want," I told him. "What's your size?"

Bill looked at me like a kid who forgot to do his homework. "Was
I supposed to know?"

"God, the men in Maybell's life . . ."

I recognized the salesgirl behind the counter from my school. She
was a year behind me and would normally never acknowledge my existence. I could see her mind calculating how the policy of shunning me
applied in a retail setting. She decided it didn't and met my eyes as I
walked up with Bill. I'm embarrassed to tell you it actually felt good to
be looked at.

"You think this guy's a medium?" I asked, pointing at Bill.

She shrugged and looked back down at her phone.

"Fine," I declared to Bill. "You're a medium."

I went through the men's section and picked out pants, tee shirts, button-downs, sweatshirts, underwear, socks and a hoodie. In a few minutes I had practically a whole wardrobe in my arms.

"Here, try these on."

Bill looked confused. "Why?"

"Make sure they fit. See if you like 'em."

Bill hesitated, and I was out of patience.

"Fine." I put the whole heap by the register. "We'll take this," I told the girl. She looked at the pile like it was three feet of shit she had to bury. She grudgingly put down her phone and picked up a scanner.

"I don't need all these clothes," Bill declared.

The girl paused mid-scan, barely concealing her annoyance.

"I told you, Maybell's payin'. Take 'em."

"I'm not going to be here that long."

I looked at Bill. That was news to me.

"If I stay too long," he added, "I might get caught up. I don't want to be stuck here."

I was surprised to find someone who seemed to hate Hadley as much as I did.

"Does Maybell know?"

Bill shook his head.

So what if Maybell loses her cook? That was her problem.

"You know what I think?" I said. "Take the whole bunch. Maybell wants to buy you clothes. It'll make her happy."

It wouldn't make her happy. It would make her pissed. That would make me happy. I handed the salesgirl Maybell's card.

"Do you get a commission on this?"

"No," she said, annoyed to be reminded.

I smiled for the first time that afternoon.

We left the store with two huge shopping bags. As we passed the food court, Bill wanted to have a look. This trip had already laid waste to my mall survival system and I was about to tell him "no." Then I heard a voice calling.

"Belutha! Belutha!"

It was Rodney coming up fast. "Shit," I turned to Bill. "I hope you can fight."

I stood between Rodney and Bill. I wasn't planning to protect Bill, just slow Rodney down a bit.

"Who in the hell is this?" Rodney asked, pointing at Bill.

"This is Bill, Rodney. And mind your own business."

"Who the hell is Bill?" Rodney reached past me and gave Bill a little shove.

"Leave, Rodney!"

"You pass me up for him? I thought we had something!"

"You and what psychedelic drug?"

Rodney slipped past me and put his face right in Bill's.

"You hear the way she talks to me, Bill?"

"Rodney!"

He wasn't listening to me now. He was getting ready to take Bill apart like an old engine.

"Whatta you doin' with my girl?"

"Dammit Rodney, I'm not your girl!"

"You hear that, Bill?" Rodney gave Bill a shove. "She's not my girl. Thanks to you!"

Bill closed his eyes. I thought he just didn't want to see the beating he was about to get. I think Rodney thought that too. But Bill wasn't afraid. He was breathing, steadily in and out. After a couple of moments, he opened his eyes and looked at Rodney. "You're angry, Rodney."

Rodney's face was half an inch from Bill's. "You know, Bill, I am. What are you gonna do about it?"

"It hurts. Belutha turned you down and now she shows up at the mall with some other guy?"

Rodney curled his lips as that sunk in. "Yeah, she did."

"It doesn't seem fair, does it? There's nothing wrong with you. Lots of girls would love to go with you. You don't go with any of them, even though you could. You *know* Belutha's the one for you. You've known it since you were little. But does she care you feel that way?"

Rodney stood still for a few moments, as if Bill had just hit him. Then he turned to me. I was surprised to see the hurt on his face.

"Well, do ya?" he said.

I stared at them both.

Bill continued, "She'd know you're perfect for her if she'd just open her damn eyes."

Rodney turned to me again and gave me an exasperated look.

"How long does she expect you to wait around? Does she think you're made of stone?"

Rodney backed up and let that wash over him. He blew out a sigh though pursed lips and then he did something I have never seen a man do: shook his fingers like they were hot. I was going to say something, but Rodney held out his hand. "I need a minute," he said.

There were small plates of food from Sbarro Pizza, Panda Express, Hot Dog On A Stick, and Mongolian Barbecue. It was Maybell's money, so I told Bill to splurge. He tried the corn dog first and didn't seem too thrilled. Rodney was eating a plate of pork-fried rice. I had nothing. Just being this close to mall food felt like a health hazard.

Rodney was mulling something over. "So you're saying back off?"

Bill nodded as he tried his egg roll. He liked that a lot more.

"But what about in the movies?" Rodney asked. "The guy always grabs the girl and—you know—kisses her." Rodney looked over at me and I could see that he was thinking about it.

"You'll be dead before you leave your seat," I said flatly.

Rodney sighed and turned back to Bill. "You see what I'm dealing with here?" Rodney grew reflective. "Maybe it's like that coffee mug. 'Let her go and she'll come back to you.'"

"I ain't coming back to you, Rodney."

"Well, that's what you say now." Rodney winked at Bill, like they shared a secret, the kind shared only among men. Bill moved onto his pizza, Rodney back to his rice. It's like I wasn't there anymore.

I stood at the kitchen door, looking at the backyard. Bill was out there, staring up at the stars the way he did that first night and every night since. The night sky seemed to be his personal TV show.

I heard Oren shouting in the living room.

"Belutha? Belutha! What the hell is this?"

He held up my book: *Lesbian Thought*.

"You went into my room?!"

"Hell, yeah, I did!"

I tried to snatch it from him, but he was too fast.

"The sign has two words, Oren. 'Keep out.' I don't know how to make it any simpler for your child brain!"

"You're too young to be a lesbo!"

I've noticed that some men fear lesbianism the way doctors fear Ebola, as if one case could lead to a global outbreak.

"I'm studying to be one so's I won't ever be sexually dependent on men scum like you."

I was glad to see that stung him. Maybell came in from the kitchen. Sonny Boy was on the couch and Clover was in the crib by his side. Sonny Boy had his headphones on, which he usually wore to block out the sound of me and Maybell arguing.

Oren turned to Maybell. "You see what your daughter's reading?"

Maybell looked at the book and tossed it aside.

"Belutha's old enough to decide her own sexual preference. Same as me."

Maybell kissed Oren on the lips and used her hand to seduce him in a way I will not ruin your day recounting. She leaned back and smiled. "Care to buy me a drink, mister?"

Oren wasn't quite done pretending to be a father. "May . . ."

She kissed him again and now his paternal work was forgotten. She led him into her bedroom and closed the door.

I yelled after them, "Don't forget your diaphragm! It's in the top drawer next to the *spermicide*!!" I picked up my book and threw it at the door.

I went to the back door and looked out. I thought for sure Bill would have heard the shouting. If he did, he didn't show it. He kept staring up at the stars as if nothing that happened in this world would ever touch him.

The diner was usually pretty quiet at eight-thirty on a Saturday morning, but this was something different. People were reading that article about Bill—some on their phones, some had bought the actual *Herald Examiner*. Harold had blogged for them before, but this was the first time they printed something of his on actual paper.

The place was quiet as a church. No one asked for refills.

Marguerite sat at the counter across from Maybell, both of them reading off their phones. Marguerite made a face at something and held her phone out. Maybell read what was on it, then looked over at Bill. He was reading the article in the newspaper that Radd was sharing with him. Maybell hoped for some expression from Bill, some kind of indignation. But there was none.

Finally, one of the other Unwise Men broke the silence.

"Bill, you tell 'em this shit?"

"Of course he didn't," someone at a table said. "This is the same newspaper that says Elvis is alive."

"Elvis *is* alive," Radd said. "I got him stayin' above my garage."

Bill took a sip of coffee and kept reading.

Maybell looked around. She had been having a good run with Bill as her cook and didn't want it to end. She asked Marguerite pretty loudly, so everyone would hear, "Didn't you say once they make shit up to sell papers?"

Marguerite got what Maybell was going for. "Yeah," she said—loudly too. "Harold said they do that all the time."

Radd turned to Bill. "You can probably sue their asses off, Bill."

"My cousin sued a mechanic," that other Unwise Man added. "The guy left a metal filing in the regulator and the engine seized up. I can give you his number."

Radd held out the newspaper. "What about it, Bill? You tell 'em this crazy shit?"

Bill frowned and picked up the paper thoughtfully. He noticed some people looking at him. He could feel their concern.

Finally, he turned to Radd. "What part do you think is crazy?"

Dead silence. Then suddenly Radd started laughing. He chucked Bill on the shoulder. The mood in the diner started to lift. A few others laughed. Radd held out his cup. "May, how 'bout a refill?"

And just like that, the diner was a diner again. People were talking and eating.

There was a *ding* as the front door opened. A family entered, sub-urban-dressed, far from home. The mom spoke up. "Excuse me, is this the diner where you get your orders mind-read?"

Maybell stood up and got back into waitress mode. "It is that. Welcome! Dolene honey, why don't you show these folks to a table?"

Dolene picked up a stack of menus and went to seat the family. Maybell took the newspaper out of Bill's hand, folded it and laid it on the counter by Radd.

"Break's over."

By noon, Maybell's parking lot was the fullest it had ever been. People managed to squeeze in some more spaces, one on either side of the propane tank, two by the dumpster. The article brought in a few more locals, but most newcomers were from out of town.

One of them drove up in an '87 sky-blue Oldsmobile Cutlass. His name was Martin Mancosa. He was somewhere in his seventies, though I couldn't tell you exactly where because at a certain point old people pretty much all look the same. He wore a mustard yellow cardigan sweater with dark wood buttons. His shirt was buttoned to the top, as if showing his neck would be considered indecent. He had both the look and smell of academia.

The article about Bill was open on his passenger seat. There were sections underlined in red, like it was a paper he had graded. He slowly squeezed his yacht of a car into a dinghy-sized parking space and got out, folding the newspaper under his arm.

He went up to the entrance, but there was a cluster of people forming, and he had to wait.

Inside the diner, it was getting very loud. For the first time since Maybell had owned it, every seat was taken.

She brought an armload of plates to a family of four. The family stared at their meals, having for the first time experienced a human being looking into their hearts and minds to cook for them what they wanted. To them it was wondrous. Maybell barely had time to say "Enjoy your meal" before moving on.

You would think not having to take people's orders would make life easier for a waitress. But Maybell noticed pretty quickly that, without a written check, she had no way of knowing what to charge her customers. So she and Dolene took to making notes on their pads of what meals they served as they dropped them off. The new routine was taking some getting used to.

At table 6, a family with three kids and a baby sat with their heads bent in prayer, saying grace. An older couple at table 9 paused after a few bites. They held each other's hands for no particular reason. The waitresses were too busy to notice any of this. Dolene had to deal with a family from Gillette in the front that couldn't find where to sit.

"I'm sorry, folks," she said. "I got no tables."

The father replied, "Where's the line?"

Maybell was refilling coffee nearby and heard that. She and Dolene met eyes. This was another first.

"Why don't you folks stand by the gumball machine," Maybell said. "We'll seat ya soon as we can."

There was no time to mark the moment. A man motioned to Dolene for a check, and Maybell had to clear booth 2. To her chagrin, she found Rose already sitting down.

"Rose," Maybell said stacking up the dishes, "You can't take a booth."

Rose kept her posture straight. "I believe this was still America last time I checked."

"I'm in peak here, Rose. I can sit you at the counter."

"I'm a reg'lar customer, and I'll sit where I reg'lary sit."

Maybell could see Rose was not going to move. "I had a cat like you once," she said, stacking the last plates. "I put her to sleep."

Maybell turned to go, but Rose stopped her. "Excuse me, I haven't given you my order."

"Rose, Bill—"

"I am not going to have my order mind-read. I want it taken the reg'lar way."

Maybell laid down the dishes with a clang and took out her pad.

At the grill, Bill must have had sixteen orders going at once. How he kept it all in his head, I will never know. He didn't even have checks on the spindle for guidance. His body moved like a dancer's, gliding from one spot to another across the grill, flipping this, pouring that.

Two of the Unwise Men had left, but Radd was still at the counter, ready with an encouraging word.

Dolene glided up to the grill. Bill pointed to a growing stack of prepared plates.

"Table 5." He indicated each plate: "Father. Mother. Boy. Girl." Dolene nodded and went. There was no time for anything else.

Then, for the first time that morning, Bill heard the metallic creak of the spindle. He looked up in surprise. Maybell put an order up.

"Don't worry about Rose," she said. "She doesn't want you to guess her order." Maybell motioned to three plates. "Table 2?"

Bill nodded. "Man. Bald man. Woman."

Maybell took the plates and hurried off. Bill took the order off the spindle and looked at it.

This is what Bill told me later. I can't say I fully understand it. But I'll tell it to you as best as I can.

He said there were always at least two realities going on all the time. There's the one most of us know, which has tables and chairs and silverware and other people. He said that's perfectly legitimate. But there are other realities about which we don't know.

As an example, he told me what was going on in the diner that day.

In what Bill called reality #1, he was a grill cook, stirring eggs, flipping burgers and such. But what was much more interesting was something he called reality #2. In that reality he described a very thin, glowing string that was connected to his body and not visible in reality #1. He said that when he wanted to guess orders, it went from him to the customers at the diner. The string was new to Bill, as new as having a body for the string to connect to. So he wasn't exactly sure how it worked. He didn't tell it what to do. He didn't say, "Hey, String, go check out that older couple from East Hadley." The string just did what needed to be done, kind of the way our legs start walking when we want to go across the street.

While he was busy guessing orders, that string crisscrossed the diner every which way, yet when Maybell and Dolene or any customers passed through it, the string stayed intact.

It was that string, in reality #2, that enabled Bill to know what people wanted to eat.

Then there was something he called reality #2.5. He used the example of Rose.

He said the string reached out to Rose that day, sitting in the booth. And that, though his body never left the grill and his right hand still held the spatula, in the time it takes to draw a breath—a lot less time than that actually—Bill felt himself sitting in that booth across from Rose. If Rose had had eyes to see reality #2.5, she would have glimpsed a flash of Bill on the other side of her table.

In that momentless moment, Bill said he could feel her need, her fears, her anguish, and her longing. Others came to the diner for a meal, and it was all pretty straightforward. But Rose came to get some relief from her pain. When Bill felt that pain, when he understood what she lived with day in and day out, year after year, he was overcome by a new desire, something he never felt before. He wanted to lessen it.

A table had cleared, and Dolene waved a family over, leaving them with a stack of menus as they sat. The menus were a formality she still hadn't shaken off. Next on the line that now stretched outside was Martin Mancosa. He was overwhelmed by the noise and the waitresses darting by. He looked all around the diner until he saw Bill. Martin absently touched the newspaper under his arm.

That was around the time that I got there. I had Clover with me. Sometimes on Saturdays I brought him to the diner as late as noon. Usually, by that time, Maybell's had a fair amount of business. Today it was off the charts. I pushed my way past the line outside.

"Excuse me! Coming through!"

I heard someone call behind me. "There's a line here, you know!"

I turned back. "You're proud to admit you're on a line for a diner?"

I squeezed my way through the door. Maybell was clearing dishes nearby.

"Jesus, Maybell!"

"Tell me about it. I need you, baby."

"Seriously?" If she thought I was going to work in that diner, my mom had a fragile grasp on reality.

"We're up to our eyeballs!" She picked up a stack of plates.

I went behind the counter to get the bubble walker. "Tell your eyeballs I'd rather get hit by a speeding bus."

I noticed Bill at the grill. In this hurricane of a diner, he worked fast but calmly, as if unbothered by the noise of it all. It made me think of him looking up at the stars.

"Hey," I said.

"Hey," he said back, a slight smile on his face. I was surprised by how much I liked seeing that.

I strapped Clover into the bubble walker. "You be good now," I told him. "Don't let them feed you any of this diner crap." An older woman nearby gave me a disapproving look. I returned the favor.

I was on my way out when I heard some commotion to my left.

Maybell had just dropped off a plate to Rose and was walking away when Rose snapped at her.

"Excuse me Miss, this isn't what I ordered."

Maybell was already setting silver down at another table. "Miss? You don't know my name by now? You practically live here."

"Maybell." Rose snapped back. "This isn't what I ordered."

Maybell went back to the booth. "Rose, I got no time for this."

As Maybell fished out the check from her pocket, Rose took a look at the unwanted plate before her. Two eggs over hard, buttered biscuits, tomato juice, grilled onions. Slowly, a deep memory was coming back to her. Something she hadn't thought about in decades.

Maybell looked at the check and came to the same conclusion as Rose. She looked back at the grill with annoyance. "I'm sorry, Rose."

But Rose was fixed on the plate. "Oh, my . . . ," she said sadly.

"It's just a mix up. I'll get your order right away."

"Jessie . . ." Rose muttered this to herself. "Oh, my Lord . . ."

Rose's parents had taught her you can't control what happens to you in this life. There will be terrible droughts. Markets will crash. People will do cruel things that surprise you. The one thing you have control over is your dignity. If you don't give it up, then no one will ever be able to take it from you.

Rose struggled mightily to maintain that dignity and for the first time since she was a child, she knew she was going to lose it. She tried to resist her curiosity, but she was powerless and had to peek under the eggs. There she found them: two slices of lightly grilled Canadian bacon.

"Oh, Jessie . . ." she heard the words erupt from her mouth. The sound of it surprised her. She had no strength left to stop herself. "I been trying to go on. I really have. I go out every day, but when I come home it's just so empty. I sleep in the den 'cause the bed don't smell like you anymore. Jessie, I think I'm losing my mind."

Her voice came out like a wail. The tables nearby had gone quiet, and that caused the rest of the diner to quiet down. I stopped by the door to watch.

Dolene leaned in close to Maybell. "Wasn't Jessie her husband?"

Maybell nodded. "Gone, I don't know how many years."

Rose looked up at Maybell, eyes filled with tears. "This was his favorite. I made it for him almost every morning. Damn bacon wouldn't keep the week."

Rose kept looking at Maybell, as if searching for something. Instinctively, Maybell put an arm around her shoulder and that was all it took. Rose started weeping into Maybell's apron.

Martin stood just behind me, as transfixed as I was.

I looked over and saw Bill. He was watching Rose and Maybell. He made the slightest nod, like a player who just hit a long ball. And then he turned to the grill and got back to work.

An hour later, people passed by the sky-blue Oldsmobile Cutlass on their way to and from the diner, paying no attention to the old man inside. Martin had been waiting for the medication to take hold and could finally feel the weakness in his muscles dissipating. He didn't mind it now. He didn't mind anything. He felt sure he'd finally found what he was looking for.

"We come from the same place—not that you can use the word 'place.' Before you were Harold and I was Bill, we both were. Really, the only difference between us is that you believe in being Harold and I don't believe in being Bill. That's because you were born and I wasn't.

"When you're born, you agree to be fully immersed. You have to believe in being Harold completely. That means no memory of who you were and what you knew before you became Harold.

"If you hadn't forgotten all that, you'd probably be mind-reading orders too."

—Bill Bill, Interview at Maybell's Diner

The girl stared at the TV as if she was looking through the wrong end of a telescope. It seemed small and distant. Some women on the show were praising a new exercise machine and the inches it took off their waistlines. They showed off the tape measures again and again, comparing before and after. It doesn't get more scientific than that, they said.

The girl didn't know what time it was. Her arm was too heavy to reach for her phone, even if she wanted to check. The shades were drawn, as they always were, to discourage nosy neighbors. That suited the girl. The house was her cocoon. Whatever lay outside held nothing she wanted.

Her housemates were either at work or out of town. Two of them were a couple she barely knew and who kept to themselves. Then there was Gus, who was on the lease, friends with Peter from way back. The other room had belonged to Peter. Now it was hers. Gus was cool to let her stay.

With the house empty like this, she could imagine herself being completely alone on the planet. That's when she felt safest.

On TV the same tape measure was measuring the same waists. And they were showing the same moves on the exercise machine. How many times were they going to make their damn point? She would love to have changed the channel, but the repetition became hypnotic, making her body feel even heavier. The effort to move was greater than the pain of watching.

She heard the front door open. It slowly came back to her that she had asked the guy to get a cappuccino from 7-Eleven. That seemed like years ago. And now suddenly it felt like he had come back way too soon. She appreciated that he would go out and get her things. She knew that when he said he loved her more than anything, he meant it. That's why she let him have sex with her. But never when she wasn't high. When she was high, she felt like she was thirty feet away from her own body, which put him thirty feet away from her. But even that became too close. She spent half her time thinking up ways to get him out of the house.

The guy took the cappuccino from the paper bag and placed it just beyond her reach. She didn't bother about it, though she was ready to offset her mellow with a little buzz. She liked this bubble feeling and wanted to keep it going.

The guy reached into his pants and pulled out other freebies he'd snatched. He never spent money without nabbing some free shit. There were two candy bars, a newspaper, a little squeezie toy. He grinned when he pulled out a can of Reddi-wip. The first squirt would be for her cappuccino. The rest was for whippets.

He laid a glob out for her and put the cup within an inch of her fingers. As she lifted her heavy body, he pulled the cup just out of reach and grinned.

"Cyril!"

She reached further this time, and he pulled the cup away again, snorting like he had made a great joke. She rolled her eyes, and he placed the cup right in her grip.

"Fucking grow up, Cyril."

He cleared the nozzle and held the can just so, to huff a good swallow of nitrous.

He held out the can to her. She wasn't ready to offset her high. The whippet would probably make him horny, and she still needed her thirty-foot buffer. Instead she reached for the *Herald Examiner* he snatched.

"Suit yourself," he said and took another gulp of nitrous.

She heard him breathing and then giggling. But it didn't matter. Nothing mattered. Suddenly there was only one thing that existed in the world. She was staring at a photo in the newspaper of some grill cook who could mind-read orders. The planet was spinning insanely under her.

"Peter . . . ," she said. A rush of pain and shock washed over her. Then a tidal wave of relief.

"He's alive?"

"Who's alive?" Cyril asked, sitting back to enjoy his buzz.

Katie didn't answer. She was looking away, toward the front

window. She noticed a thin sliver of light on the edge of the curtain. So it was still day outside. For the first time since forever, it seemed, she wanted to go out into it.

O ren dipped the piston in warm grease and stroked it gently in an up and down motion. He inserted the clean shaft slowly into its socket, the excess grease oozing out and dripping down. He enjoyed the virility of his mighty machine.

Oren had a lot of time to care for his Harley. His secret to life was low overhead. The lower your expenses, the less you had to do to meet them. He had a two-pronged approach to his philosophy, which was one prong more than I thought a guy like Oren was capable of.

His first prong was expenses and keeping them low. After his sperm violated me in egg form, and once Maybell's belly became less than perfectly flat, Oren saw the open horizon of his life being cut off by 2x4, dry wall and screaming babies. So he took off one dark morning while Maybell slept, without a note or warning. Maybell didn't see or hear from him for almost a year. He met a girl in Tulsa and stayed with her most of that time—rent free, by the way. When, after a while, that girl starting talking marriage, Oren saw the 2x4 and dry wall closing in again and hit the road.

Around that time, Oren began to sense a great possibility he felt other men hadn't yet discovered. Women would put him up for a while, which was fine because a while was all he wanted with them. Eventually, the subject would turn to putting down roots and having babies, and so Oren would hit the road and be free again. Almost every time this happened, after every new woman and new escape, he found his way back to Maybell. There's no one like your first. He would have actually loved Maybell, had he been capable of such a feeling. In truth, he just missed the familiarity and the smell. He'd stay until the smell got too strong and the familiarity reminded him of why he left. And then he'd slip away into the night.

Oren's second prong was really simple. He knew the Harley inside and out and would sometimes rebuild one for a rich guy. Or a guy with enough money to pretend he was rich. Oren didn't have to do it often to get the small income he needed for basics. And besides, he liked the work. He was always tinkering with his own Harley just because.

He was doing it now outside of Maybell's house when he saw a Ford Escort approach from down the road. It pulled over, and its lame engine sputtered before it stopped. Oren showed his contempt for the Escort by not looking up.

Rose stepped out and approached the house, a bag in her hand. She looked as out of place as she felt. Oren kept working, even as she stepped up to him.

"Uh, excuse me," Rose said. "Is this, uhm, do you know if this is Maybell Mariah's house?"

"Who's askin'?" Oren didn't look up.

Rose tried to explain, "Well, earlier, you see Bill said I should . . ."

Oren caught a glimpse of Rose and suddenly lit up. "Hey, I know you. Didn't you work in the library back when?" Before Rose could answer, he went on. "Yeah! We used to call you the Church Lady. 'Well, isn't that special!'" Oren cracked himself up while Rose just stood there.

Inside the kitchen, Bill was cutting vegetables and starting to cook in pots and pans that had gone so long unused, I didn't even know we had them. I guessed they must have come with the house. In my sixteen-plus years of life, this was the first real dinner cooked there.

I found a small patch of free space on the counter and sat there to watch. Sonny Boy wasn't interested, but I was curious to see how it was a kitchen gets used. I was especially curious after that day at the diner.

Bill had a chicken and some potatoes roasting in the oven. That was another first. Maybell had used the oven to dry clothes once or twice, but otherwise she relied on the micro.

When he opened the oven door, I felt a wave of heat and I was hit by a smell I can only describe as homey. For the first time, I understood why some people associate home with comfort. Bill dipped a spoon into the pan and drizzled some liquid on top of the chicken. Then he closed the oven and went back to cutting vegetables. His focus was so absolute, he had forgotten I was there. This enforced my theory about him.

"How do you know what people want to eat?" I asked. "Are you one of those idiot savants, like *Rain Man*?"

Bill looked at me for a second, but before he could process that question, he realized he had forgotten the parsley. He opened the fridge and pulled out the bag of greens, adding it to the mix.

"I guess you wouldn't know if you were," I went on, "'cause technically you'd be an idiot."

The doorbell rang and Bill rushed out eagerly.

"That must be it," I thought.

Rose was at the door when Bill opened it. He motioned for her to come in. "Rose, glad you came!"

She looked around tentatively. "I didn't know if I should bring something." She handed Bill a bag with store-bought cookies.

I came out from the kitchen and must have been staring because Rose grew uneasy when she looked at me. I had seen her at the diner plenty of times and had nothing against her. My mind was just not able to grasp what she was doing in my house.

"This is Belutha," Bill said. "That's Sonny Boy over there and next to him, that's Clover," Bill turned to us. "Rose is here for dinner."

Sonny Boy went back to his game.

"I have to cook, Rose. Make yourself at home."

I gave Rose another leery look and followed Bill back into the kitchen. She just stood in place, like a girl who'd been sent to the principal.

Sonny Boy stared at the TV, as if she wasn't there. I suppose for him, she wasn't. So Rose stepped up to the crib. The baby looked up at her. He wasn't quite fussy, but she could tell he had some fussiness coming on.

"How old is he?" she asked. Sonny Boy just shrugged.

Rose hesitated. It wasn't her place, she knew. But babies need attention and that's all there was to it. She picked up Clover and held him in the crook of her arm. She was surprised at how quickly it all came back to her, as if the last thirty-five years were just one breath. She bounced Clover lightly, telling him what a good boy he was. She had seen him almost every day in the diner, waddling around in his bubble walker. And now having watched him at Sonny Boy's side, with his mother behind her closed bedroom door, Rose realized just how infrequently this baby had been held.

She had two grandchildren herself, living with her divorced son, Rory, and his girlfriend somewhere in Europe. When Rory was a boy, he and Jessie fought pretty much every day. She used to say the two of them were like combustible chemicals that should never be mixed. Rory had joined the Army the moment he was old enough, for no reason except to spite his father. He was overseas in Afghanistan when his first baby was born. Jessie was already dead by then, and still Rory didn't so much as send Rose a picture. He may have hated his father, but he had plenty of blame leftover for Rose. Last she heard, Rory and his kids were in Germany. She had still never met her grandchildren.

Rose walked around the living room to give Clover a view that babies don't get from a crib. But instead of looking around, he kept his eyes fixed on her. They were clear blue and hardly blinked. Looking at them, Rose felt a pain in her chest like a hammer had struck it. It was so strange and alien that it took a few moments before she realized that it wasn't pain at all. It was joy.

She thought: How did I live all these years without holding a baby?

Bill added some soup stock to the veggies. I was sitting on the counter again. I wanted to ask him why on earth he would invite an old lady to the house, but I had something more important on my mind.

"I read that article," I said. "Says you were never born. You kind of entered a body that was already dead. They made that up—right?"

Bill stopped a moment, shook his head, then went back to cooking.

"No? So you told 'em that?"

Bill nodded.

"And you told 'em that because . . . You were messing around?"

Bill shook his head again. His mind was mostly fixed on what he was cooking.

"You're sayin' it's true? You were never born?"

Bill looked at me. He knew this was a loaded subject and I could see he was uncomfortable. "Yeah," he finally said.

"So what, you just sprung up off a bed in a hospital inside some other guy's dead body?"

"Uh-huh."

He went back to cooking. So there it was. Maybell hired a crazy guy who was making dinner for all of us in her kitchen. Maybe that's why he was able to know what people wanted before they ordered. It's like he was missing some screws in his head, but then had some other screws most of us didn't have. At least that's what made sense at the time.

When I watched him cook, I was struck by how complete his attention was. Bill had no sense of insecurity or self-consciousness as far as I could see. He was fully devoted to whatever he was doing, with no thought for anything else. And there was a grace to the way he moved. Nothing was rushed. Everything was deliberate.

He didn't mind the silence, or me watching him. Which only made me want to watch him more. Finally, I broke the silence.

"Are you an alien?"

"Aliens are born. They're just born somewhere else."

"So you were never born, period? What have you got against being born? It's good enough for everyone else."

Bill grew thoughtful. "I don't think it would make sense to you."

"Try me."

Bill stopped cooking and turned to me. "Okay, so you're born. It's a new life—right? You're a new person. Never existed before?" He paused.

"Are you asking me?"

Bill nodded.

"Yeah, I never existed before."

He smiled.

"What? What, Bill?"

"That's how it works. You're not supposed to remember," he said.

"Remember what?"

"Before."

"Before what? Before I was born? That's nuts."

Bill gave me a knowing look, then went back to cooking.

"Okay I get it. I can't remember what it is I can't remember. That's a bit of Jedi mind-trick, Bill."

Sure he was crazy, I thought, but there was some logic to it.

"You're sayin' I did exist. I don't know 'cause I forgot. But you didn't forget, 'cause why? You didn't come out of someone's birth canal?"

Bill nodded in a way to say, "That's sort of it."

I watched him in silence for a bit. I couldn't explain it, but I felt safe with Bill. Who cared that Maybell hired a crazy guy. Maybe we were all kind of crazy. I figured you had to be to live in this world.

Oren went into the bathroom and stopped short when he saw Rose kneeling by the tub. She was bathing Clover.

"What the hell?"

"Oh, don't mind me," Rose said. "Seemed like ages since this baby had a bath."

"Geez," Oren muttered. He went to the sink to clean the grease off his hands.

Rose rinsed off Clover and pulled up the stopper. She stood to pick up the baby.

"Open up that towel over there, would ya?"

Oren rolled his eyes and did as he was asked. Rose put the baby into the towel in such a way that forced Oren to hold it under its arms.

"Just pat him dry," she said, turning to dry her own hands.

Oren stood motionless, as if Rose had just handed him a ticking bomb.

"I don't take care'a babies."

"No. You just make 'em."

Rose snatched up Clover and gave Oren a disapproving look.

Oren needed some old biddy sneering at him like he needed a hole in his oil pan. He wiped his still greasy hands and stepped out into the living room. He found his way blocked by Sonny Boy, standing now to play his video game.

"D'ya mind?" Sonny Boy took a step back and Oren squeezed by him. He shook his head and sighed loudly in case Sonny Boy couldn't tell he was displeased.

Oren entered Maybell's room and found a mess of clothes all over the bed.

"Dammit, Maybell, is this a house or a damn train station?"

"Train station," she said. "Tickets, please." She brushed her hand on Oren's crotch and then went back to organizing. "Take a look," she said. "I cleared out a drawer for you. Now you don't have to keep your clothes balled up in your bag."

Maybell didn't stop and look at the expression on Oren's face. If she had, she might have noticed his knitted brow. He was starting to feel that 2x4 and dry wall closing in around him.

Martin had no idea how long he'd been awake. He'd gotten used to some insomnia, but this new medication made it ridiculous. When he opened his eyes again he could see a wash of gray peeking from under the motel curtains. He let out a sigh, resigned that his night's sleep was done.

Martin was staying at the Hadley 8 out on Route 32. He was the first of the pilgrims who came because of Bill's cooking. Others that came after stayed at the 8 or at Emma's RV Park.

Until about a year and a half ago, Martin had been a professor at Briar College. He was chairman of the philosophy department, though it was hard to call it a department since he was the only full-time professor.

Martin was raised by two academics who valued intellect above all else. By fifteen, Martin was an avowed atheist. He had a sense of reverence, but not for God. It was for the Great Ideas, the philosophies of the ages as he called them. While a professor, he tried to instill that reverence in his students. Why look to an outside deity when there was meaning to be found in human reason?

Then a pain in his leg brought him to the doctor and he learned about a form of cancer he couldn't even pronounce. It had already moved to his bones and would stay there until it killed him.

Martin suddenly found himself falling into an abyss that had no light and no end. There was not a single Great Idea that could save him. The pointlessness of life was rising up to envelop him in darkness. He was terrified.

So he set out to find some reason behind it all, an alternative to the nothing he believed in. Something he could live with and die with. He gave up his position at Briar and hit the road. He drove to the Midwest to talk with evangelists—not the charlatans you see on TV, but people of real faith. He spent a month living at a spiritual community in Santa Fe and another at the Self-Realization Fellowship. He had long debates with a channeled spirit named Gossamer and another known only as The Teacher. He sat in meditation circles holding out his arms to accept the Light. But while those around him basked in the glow, Martin remained in darkness.

Then, in a Coffee Bean & Tea Leaf just outside Berkley, among the newspapers on a bench next to him, he saw a copy of the *Herald Examiner*. The story about Bill caught his eye. Martin was more than desperate by that point and willing to try anything. He got in his car and set out for Hadley.

He had been floored by what he saw in the diner the day before. The excitement had cost him, and he'd spent the last twelve hours on his back. But he was rested now. He sat up in bed, determined that today he was going to talk to Bill.

The mighty man stepped into the cool pre-dawn air. Oren loved traveling when others slept. It kept him ahead of them all. Who could understand the mighty man? Who could predict his moves?

Not Maybell.

She was in bed when she stirred and felt the emptiness next to her. She knew immediately what it meant. It had always hurt, but for some reason this time it hurt more. Maybe it was the pain of an empty bed that she could no longer stand. She buried her face in Oren's pillow, breathed in his scent and then let out a moan like an animal in mourning. It filled the house.

Oren got on his Harley. The metal was cold, but would warm up soon. He started the engine, reliable as always. Then he looked back at the house and was taken by surprise.

I was standing there. I held my rifle, and it was aimed at him.

He cut the engine and slowly got off the bike. "Belutha, honey. . . . Put the rifle down."

He took a step toward me. I leveled the barrel. I had his forehead in my sight.

"Shh," I said. "Listen. You hear that?"

From inside the house came the painful sound of Maybell moaning. It actually made me feel sorry for her.

"You hear what you do to her?"

Oren kept his hands in the air. "I can't help that."

"I suppose I can't help it if I shoot you."

"Belutha . . ."

I hated when he used my name. It seemed foul coming from his mouth. I shot at the ground six inches from his boot.

"Dammit!"

"Oh, I'm sorry," I said. "You see, I just can't help myself."

I fired again, hitting a rock near his other boot, sending fragments flying. He covered his eyes.

Without rushing, I reached into my robe pocket and pulled out two more rounds. I heard him coming at me. I could see him out of the corner of my eye. I didn't care at all. Let him take the rifle and shoot me. It's all the same.

I just got the rifle loaded when Oren was close enough to grab the barrel. He pulled the rifle out of my hands and swung it back to hit me with the stock. I could see how badly he wanted to. I have to give him credit for stopping himself. In one motion he let the barrel fall into his left hand and he brought his right hand down on my face hard. An open palm, but it felt like a punch.

I didn't flinch. I kept staring right at him, daring him to club me with the rifle. I would never be afraid of him. Not ever.

I heard the front door open and knew without looking that Maybell was there along with Bill and Sonny Boy. I didn't take my eyes off Oren.

"Don't you come 'round here no more," I told him. "All you ever bring is pain."

Maybell came up to stand by my side and put her arm around my shoulder. She was too broken up to say anything.

There was silence. Oren looked around and then back at me. I had ruined his clean exit.

"You got a lot ta learn about this world, young lady. A man can't help who he is."

"You're giving me a life lesson now? You think talking to me like you're my daddy makes you some kind of father?"

I pressed forward and felt Maybell's arm keeping back.

"I bet you carry a picture of me in your wallet," I said. "Show it to the whores you meet. Does it make 'em wanna fuck you?"

Oren's jaw tensed up. He took his wallet from his back pocket and pulled out a picture of me from when I was about eleven. He tore it up, keeping his eyes on mine, then put the wallet back. He turned and got on his Harley.

He started it up with a roar to wake the dead and drove off without looking back.

I turned to go in the house. Bill and Sonny Boy stepped aside to let me through. As the door closed I glanced back outside and could see Maybell kneeling down, starting to pick up the pieces of my picture.

Bill didn't realize his legs had brought him out to the back of the house. His mind was distracted, and it wasn't until he noticed the brightening sky going this way and that that he realized he was pacing. He had heard of pacing. He never understood the point of it until now. It kept the body occupied so that the mind was free to wander. He found it remarkable that his body could function on its own, even decide where to go, without being told what to do. He made a note to pace more often.

Since feeling Rose's pain the day before, Bill had experienced a kind of unrest that he didn't understand. Now, that morning, he'd had front row seats to my family drama. He felt downright agitated. There was no reason that anything that happened to any of the people he met should matter to him. Bill thought of us all the way a doctor might see patients in a mental hospital: whatever good qualities we possessed were offset by our psychiatric disorders. Best to keep a distance.

And yet there he was, giving a shit. Bill hadn't anticipated the powerful effect of empathy.

The sound of Maybell's voice cut through his reflections. She was calling him to come out to the truck so they could get to work.

Bill knew that life on a planet involved pain. It was one of the reasons he had shunned it for so long. But he hadn't realized that the pain of others would become almost as unbearable as his own.

By the time Bill got into the truck, his mind was made up to do something about it.

"When you're born, you give up the ability to perceive actual reality. Instead, you get sensory organs that put together a narrow picture of reality from the fragmented pieces you perceive.

"You do have other senses that don't require a physical organ. Intuition is one. Empathy is another. There aren't a fixed number of these because they vary from person to person. And the combination of these senses can work together in an almost limitless number of ways."

—Bill Bill, Interview at Maybell's Diner

There was a line stretching outside the diner. Maybell's parking lot was at capacity, and Police Chief Munt, who had just stopped by for some coffee to go, was now planted in the road directing runoff traffic to an unused stretch across Main Street. He had radioed for help, not to direct traffic, but to get his coffee.

Martin had already parked and was on the line to get in.

Inside, the diner and the people working there were at capacity. There were still a good number of regulars who weren't going to be turned away by any damn tourists. Radd had his usual stool, but the other Unwise Men refused to stand on a line and went back home.

Dolene was chagrined to see that Maybell was moving like it was a regular day, which is to say she was fast, but nowhere near fast enough to keep up. On top of that, there was a bottleneck in the system. The waitresses had to stop by the grill to ask Bill what the customers wanted to drink. Dolene thought they should limit the mind reading just to food orders. She wanted to say so, but she was an expert at reading Maybell's mood and knew to hang back.

Maybell was pouring refills when she passed a well-dressed couple who had driven in from the next county. The man held out his fork and called to get her attention.

"Excuse me, Miss, can I get another fork? This one's dirty."

Maybell stopped with her back to him. It was the kind of moment you see in Westerns, just before the gunfighter spins around and fires. Luckily, Maybell wasn't armed. She turned and walked up to the guy. Without taking her eyes off his, she took his fork from his hand, dipped it in his coffee, wiped it on her apron and put it down next to his plate.

He sat motionless under her gaze. "Thank you, Miss."

Maybell walked away. The man's wife whispered to him, "They need to find better help."

Maybell went to the grill and pointed to Bill's growing stack of cooked meals. "Table 4?"

Bill pointed to three plates: "Man. Woman. Girl."

Maybell nodded and took the plates. Bill had been keeping a close eye on her all morning, the way a parent might stand ready to grab a toddler who's teetering near the top of a staircase.

At the kitchen door, Rose stepped into the diner wearing a waitress uniform. Shortly before, when she got to the diner, Bill had waved her over and told her with absolute certainty that what she needed most in her life was to start working there. Rose hesitated only a moment. As insane as that idea seemed, it was at the same time the most sane thing she had ever heard. She had no idea why.

Now, entering from the kitchen, she found herself behind the counter. In all the years she had been eating there, she had never once seen the diner from that vantage point. It seemed strange to her that this place had a whole other side to it, and she had never bothered to notice it before.

She tried to tie the apron strings behind her back and discovered this to be the first insurmountable challenge of being a waitress. Bill noticed and checked the grill to make sure he had a quick moment to step away. He came up behind Rose to help.

"Are you sure about this?" she asked him.

Before he could answer, Maybell swung over. "What the hell is going on?"

"I thought you and Dolene could use some help," Bill said and then added, "Did you know Rose once worked at her college cafeteria?" He had heard Rose mention that the night before.

Maybell stared at Bill like she had never met him.

"Community college," Rose clarified. "I was in charge of Christmas decorations."

Bill pointed to the grill. "I should get back." He took off before Maybell could say anything.

Rose gave Maybell a sheepish look. "If you want, I can go back and change."

Maybell took a breath. "No, we need all the help we can get. And Lord knows you spent enough time here. Why don'cha start seatin' people?"

Outside, Maybell's former grill cook had practically taken up residence. Harley kept his truck parked there from about seven a.m., when he popped open his first beer, until closing. He had brought his own sandwiches and a bottle to pee in. Most of his day was spent sitting on his tailgate, telling anyone who would listen about the wicked man who stole his job.

One of them was Reverend Wrightwood, on his way for some breakfast with his wife.

"Harley," the Reverend said.

"Padre." Harley tipped his head and held up his beer as if in a toast.

Harley was never going to be a local success story, but the Reverend could see the man had taken a fall. "Don't you know you're playing into the devil's hands?"

"Don't gotta tell me. Saw him with my own eyes. Bill fucking Bill." Harley took a swig and added knowingly, "Like that's his real name."

Elsewhere in the parking lot, a blue Dodge pulled out, leaving an opening. A car on Main Street cut ahead of the three in front of it and snuck in before anyone noticed. It was the old red Camaro. Cyril was driving. He didn't want to be there in the worst way, but it was satisfying to beat three cars for a spot. Katie sat in the passenger seat, staring at the diner. Her expression was haunted. All this made no sense to her.

About this time, Martin Mancosa had reached the front of the line inside. The article was tucked under his arm and his eyes were on Bill. He hoped for a seat close enough to talk to him. He held out his hand to the waitress going by.

"Excuse me, Miss."

Rose snapped back, "Do I look like a 'Miss' to you?" Then she thought that part of working there might include being polite to customers. Reluctantly she pointed to an open stool. "Seat at the counter."

She walked away, feeling new admiration for Maybell for having done this job so long.

Martin took a seat. He thought that, even dressed in kitchen whites and busily flipping eggs, Bill did not look ordinary. If he hadn't read the article, Martin would still have thought there was something special about him.

No one in the diner, Martin included, had any idea what Bill was experiencing as he took a moment to look up from the grill and draw a breath. If they could have known, they would have seen something like this:

That thin, glowing string that tethered Bill to his body had crisscrossed the diner so many times that you couldn't tell where it began or ended. It retreated from customers who were leaving and reached out to those who sat down. It stopped by a family of four as they held each others' hands to pray. And went to an older couple who had moved out to the desert back in the '70s on account of his asthma.

Then it moved over to Martin. Though Bill stood twenty feet away, he was in that moment closer to Martin than anyone had ever been on earth. He knew what Martin was struggling with, in his body and in his mind. Whatever had brought most people to the diner, Martin's reason was unique.

At the grill, Bill quickly tended to a few orders until he was free to step away. He walked up to Martin, who looked up in surprise.

"The thing of it is, I can't really help you," Bill said.

Martin tried to gather his wits.

"I know what you're looking for," Bill went on, "but it won't do you any good, even if I gave you exactly what you wanted. I'm sorry."

Bill turned to walk away.

Martin reached out and put his hand on Bill's. "Please, this is so important."

Suddenly Rose came up beside Martin. "Mister, you let Bill cook or I will boot your sorry butt out that door."

Martin took his hand off Bill's. Bill gave him a smile and was about to turn away, but quickly added: "I'll get your French toast, slice of orange, no syrup."

Martin stared with his mouth open. Bill left, and Rose gave Martin a glare of warning before she went off.

Outside, Cyril was getting anxious. If he hadn't snatched that damn newspaper, how much better life would have been. After a week it would have been off the rack, and then Katie never would have seen that article. He'd have the whole rest of his life with her. He was that close, and he blew it all because he got too greedy.

The line moved up, and now he and Katie were next to go inside the diner. When Katie had insisted on coming to town, Cyril knew he had to take her. What excuse could he make for not going? Now all he needed was for Peter to let on that Cyril came before. Even threatened him. Katie would never talk to him again.

At least Cyril was prepared. Last night when he had gone upstairs to get his stuff, he snuck into Gus's room. Cyril quietly slid open the dresser drawer and took Gus's gun. It sat like a rock now in Cyril's jacket pocket. It's not that Cyril was planning to use it in front of all these people, especially with a cop out in the street. But it felt good to know it was there.

There was some movement at the front of the line inside the diner.

Cyril felt a rush of panic. On an impulse, he lit a cigarette. He even offered one to Katie, who shook her head. He was proud of himself for thinking of that last bit. It would be more convincing. And it was just in time. The whole line moved up. It was their turn to enter. He held up his lit cigarette as if to say, "What can I do?"

"Cyril?" Katie scolded.

"I'll meet you inside." He took another drag and wafted the smoke away from others on line, as if being considerate. Katie shook her head and entered the diner.

Bullet dodged.

The first crash got no attention above all the noise at the diner. Even the guys sitting at the counter barely noticed, and Maybell was right in front of them. She had been dumping dishes in the bin when a glass slipped and broke on the floor.

I like to think of Maybell that day as having been an active volcano. There had been smoke rising out of her all morning. The people who knew her saw the signs and kept their distance. That glass breaking had cracked open the mantle somewhere in Maybell's core that kept the molten lava back. Now it all came spewing out. Maybell pulled out the dish bin, flipped it over and threw it on the floor in a jumble of food and broken dishes. She smashed the empty bin on the counter over and over. The whole diner went quiet.

There was no upside to any of that. She'd be cleaning up the mess and paying for the dishes. Then again, taking a bad situation and a making it worse was Maybell's specialty.

She looked around, realizing all eyes were on her. "What the hell you all lookin' at?" she demanded, as if she was the one person there with any sense. She stormed into the kitchen.

No one noticed how rapidly Bill cleared the grill, not even Martin, who became distracted by Maybell. Bill reached for a clean glass off the shelf, filled it with ice, then found what he was looking for in the condiment cooler—a jar of sweetened cherries, the manmade color of bright red. Bill strained some of the juice into the glass and then added Coke from the soda dispenser. He found Dolene standing between him and the kitchen door.

"I wouldn't go in there if you wanna live," she said.

I guess Bill wasn't too attached to living, because he went.

Maybell was pacing around the kitchen like a wild animal in a zoo that was unable to accept captivity. She saw Bill at the door.

"Bill, get the goddam hell back to work!"

Bill gently stepped forward and put the soda on the prep table, then stepped back. Maybell was too preoccupied to pay attention.

"Goddammit!" she yelled. "Goddammit! It wasn't supposed to goddam be like this! Dammit! How the hell did my life turn to fucking shit??!"

Her pacing left her near the glass of soda and she looked down. Water was already beading on the outside and bubbles were still popping. Without really thinking, she took a sip. There was the usual sensation of bubbles down the back of her throat.

She felt her next explosion coming on. That glass would make a fine projectile and the wall behind Bill was a primo target. But then something caught in her throat. A flavor she hadn't tasted in a long time. Not since she was a kid, she realized. It was a cherry Coke. For the longest time, from when she was six until about ten, cherry Coke was her favorite drink. Her father would take her to Tom's Cafe in Prescott every time they drove there to visit his family. The place had a soda fountain, and each time they went he got her a cherry Coke.

Maybell hadn't thought of her father in years and felt ashamed for that. She didn't realize until that moment just how much comfort that man had given her. The feeling had been gone so long she had forgotten it entirely. But now it came flooding back, almost as if he had just ordered her that cherry Coke.

"When did life get so shitty?" she wondered aloud. "I'm in this hole, and I can't get out. It just gets deeper and deeper."

She took another sip. The bubbles in her throat felt so familiar. When was the last time she felt any kind of comfort, other than in a bottle or in bed with a man? But here it was, in a glass of cherry Coke. She shook her head at how easy it was to feel it after all this time. Then she remembered Bill. She was about to tell him to get back to the grill, but when she looked up he was already on his way.

Maybell turned her back to the door, to the diner and all the people in it. She leaned against the prep table and took another sip. She was going to enjoy her soda however damn long it took.

Once he saw the shift in Maybell's mood, Bill's mind had gone back to the grill. These few minutes would cost him, and he was already planning how to group-cook five orders of scrambled eggs and squeeze some extra room for hotcakes. He saw Martin was well into his French toast when he passed by the counter. Bill made a mental note to talk with Martin later.

By the time he reached the grill, Katie was close enough to the front of the line to see him. She felt her heart leap. He was alive. Right there, not twenty feet away. So much pain and torment and it was all for nothing. The whole room seemed brighter. The whole world.

And then he saw her. And he smiled. Her nightmare was over.

She walked toward the counter, still numb. But as she got closer, something strange happened. She saw that his gaze moved off her face. He hadn't been looking at her at all. He was looking at some guy who was standing on the line behind her, some guy he called "Radd."

Here's the thing about Bill in that moment. With his mind on the grill and then on Radd, he hadn't yet focused on the next customers on line. If he had, he might have known the pain this young woman was in and her absolute conviction that he alone had caused it.

Katie was just five feet away when Bill turned back to the grill as if she wasn't there. As if she wasn't even alive. Katie felt like a stake had gone straight through her heart. She was already crying as she turned to go, pushing her way past all those people waiting to get in.

Cyril watched as she walked right by him and toward the car. He hurried to catch up.

Katie banged on the passenger door and Cyril quickly unlocked it. She slammed it hard when she got in. Cyril got in next to her.

"He acted like he didn't even see me! Fucker wouldn't even look at me!" She kicked out in front of her and turned away to cry.

Cyril felt a wave of anger at the man who caused her pain. And he felt something else. It was a sense of protectiveness toward Katie. He got the girl he had dreamed of, and now he wanted to defend her. Like a knight. It felt kind of noble.

Cyril's hand rested on the gun in his pocket. He liked this new version of himself.

Bill had seared the meat on both sides and then covered it with ketchup, salt, paprika, some chili flakes, a good splash of vinegar, and a bit of sugar. He added Brussels sprouts and carrots to the baking pan, then covered it tight with aluminum foil and set it to bake at 325 degrees.

He did all that as soon as he got home because the meat needed a long time to get tender. I was in my room at the time, unaware of what Bill was up to, unaware of anything going on around me. It was one of those days that pass unnoticed, when you can't say for sure you were alive.

I know I fed and clothed a human baby that morning. And I must have ridden him on my bike to Maybell's Diner, probably zigzagging dangerously through traffic to get there. I just don't remember doing it.

I do remember a moment between fourth and fifth period. I was at my locker when some guy got right in my face and screamed at me, then laughed with his friends. That woke me up a bit. I know I went to my next class, but the class itself is a blank. I was amazed afterwards to find I had taken notes.

The reason for my non-day was Oren. I had said everything that needed saying that morning. And it's true that he was gone. But it didn't matter. He'd be back. No matter what I did or said, he'd be back, and he'd be in my life because he was in Maybell's life, and there wasn't a thing I could do about it. Oren would always win, and I would always lose.

It wasn't until late that afternoon, when the smell of cooking meat came wafting into my room, that I finally came out of my daze. I went into the kitchen and found that, even though there was practically no counter space, Bill had left a spot open for me.

So I sat in that spot, watching in silence as he set about peeling and quartering potatoes to get them boiling on the stove. Since we had some time, I decided that I would ask him some questions and try to poke a hole in his delusion.

Did Bill miss not having parents?

He didn't know what parents felt like, so no.

Did he miss having a childhood?

Same answer.

How did he know our language if he just got here?

Language is a much simpler form of communication than actual thought. Actual thought can use any language.

What does that mean, actual thought?

It's the way we think when we're not limited by being in a body.

How can someone think without a body?

It's harder to think with one.

Are there others who don't have bodies?

Yes. Every single person on earth, before coming here, didn't have a body. Bodies are a relatively new development.

How did he learn how to cook?

At first, by watching the other cook at the diner. Later, by asking the food.

Food can talk?

Not in words. It's more like he can pick up on its potential. He can tell what food can be and also what people want it to be.

Where was Bill before coming to earth?

The word "where" is kind of limiting. Not everything is situated in "where."

If it's not in a place then how can it be anywhere?

It just can.

How come Bill's the only one who gets to decide he doesn't want to be born?

He's not. Others have come the same way he did. Plus, there are many, many more who never came at all.

What happened to them, the ones who came like Bill?

Some of them came and left. Some of them stayed so long they forgot everything they knew from before. They eventually wound up living out their lives like the rest of us, until their bodies died.

When they died, did they go back to being who they were before?

Yes.

What happens when *we* die?

The same thing.

If that's the case, why bother coming here at all?

That's what he came to find out. He said it makes no sense to him either.

The potatoes were done. Bill drained the hot water and let cold water wash over them.

I had been sitting on the kitchen counter this whole time. I felt relaxed being in a room with Bill. I think it was because he was so non-invasive. There was no part of him that was out to control or get inside any part of me. Or maybe it was because, like me, Bill thought the world was kind of crazy.

But I could see he had something on his mind. It took him some effort to finally come out with it.

"Why did Oren leave?" He tried to make his voice sound casual, but Bill was new to lying. He was still bothered about that morning.

"Oren never stays anywhere long. He's basically unavailable to anyone 'cause he's already in a full-time relationship with himself."

"He barely talked to Sonny Boy."

"He's not Sonny Boy's father. That's some guy over in Gaylordville—Wayne. Oren's not Clover's dad either. Even Maybell doesn't know who that is. She stopped bothering with names a long time ago."

Bill was taking that in. I could have told him not to trouble himself. Trying to understand my family was a waste of effort.

I decided to confide something I had never admitted to anyone. "Sometimes I wish Oren and Maybell had never met. I mean, sometimes I wish I had never been born. I guess that sounds pretty messed up, huh?"

I figured if anyone might understand, it would be Bill. And he did have the slightest grin. I was about to ask him about that, when Sonny Boy came into the kitchen.

"I found another chair out back."

"Thanks," Bill said.

Sonny Boy doing anything to help anyone was another first in that house.

"You want me to set the table now?"

"Yeah. Make it for six."

Sonny Boy grabbed some plates and silverware. "Smells good," he said on the way out. I could only stare.

Bill went about rinsing a bowl for salad and got lettuce from the fridge. I had something else on my mind.

"If we all come from the same place, then how come you can mind-read orders and we can't?"

"You could."

I gave him a dubious look.

"You just have to feel what people feel."

I shook my head. "That's not really my thing."

"It's easier than you think," he said. "I'll show you how."

Maybell sat at her dresser mirror and paused.

Normally the point of this mirror was not to see her face but to cover it. To hide from herself and from the men who might help her forget—for a moment or for a night—the emptiness of her life. But now she allowed herself a view. The crow's feet. The furrows on her upper lip. They were like lines on a roadmap that went in only one direction, deeper. It was a screaming reminder of the life she never managed to get on track.

Twenty years ago she was the hottest thing that valley had produced. Even when she was my age, men put their life plans on hold while in her presence, as there was no thought produced inside a man's head that could possibly be heard above the din of Maybell. She could have had anyone she wanted and, in defiance of reason, she chose Oren.

I've seen pictures of Oren from back then, and he was actually quite the babe. He was a bad boy, which attracted her. Maybell's dad was dead set against him, which doubled his appeal. She and Oren had planned to move to California, where he was going to set up a bike shop and she was going to look golden in the sun. But my fertilization ruined all that.

Maybell picked up her phone and redialed Marguerite, getting her voicemail yet again. "Hon, it's me. Where on God's green earth are you? Call me—and I mean call me!"

Marguerite was Maybell's go-to shoulder, and Maybell was hers. There was an understanding they'd had since they were teenagers that, when a crisis came up, the other would be there. Two voicemails in a row meant 911, and the other would call back no matter what. Now Maybell was up to something like nine messages. Marguerite had gone AWOL, just as Maybell's life turned to shit.

"That girl had better have a damn good excuse," she muttered.

It didn't occur to Maybell that something could be going on with her best friend. And that, whatever it might be, it was at that moment hurtling toward Maybell with the speed and fury of a runaway train.

Maybell turned back to the mirror and proceeded to cover up her history with pancake and paint, intending to bury it along with all those painful feelings, in the arms and the smell and the pleasure of a man.

Rose had pretty much taken charge of Clover. It was only her second time visiting Maybell's home, but after just twenty-four hours she and Clover were bonded like rebar in cement. Maybell was glad to have any help she could get, especially if money wasn't involved.

When the doorbell rang, me and Bill were in the kitchen, and Rose was occupied with Clover. So Sonny Boy answered the door.

He and Martin Mancosa stared at each other, old man and young, as if across a great chasm. Neither knew what to say to the other for a long moment. Then Sonny Boy turned and yelled, "Bill! Some old guy's here!" He went back to the sofa.

Martin looked lost until Bill came in from the kitchen.

"Martin, glad you could make it. Sonny Boy, Rose, this is Martin."

Martin was disappointed to see the hostile waitress from the diner. She wasn't any happier to see him.

"Make yourself at home, Martin. Dinner's going to be ready soon." Bill started for the kitchen.

"Bill," Martin said. "I was hoping you and I could have a chance to talk."

"I know. And we will, when the time comes."

"When the time comes?"

Bill went back to the kitchen. Martin stood there a long moment, unsure of what to do. Rose motioned him over.

"You," she said. "Why don't you make yourself useful?"

Rose reminded Martin of a harsh schoolteacher. He noticed now that she was changing a baby. He was confused. Was the baby hers? No, he realized she was too old. He was trying to run through all the possible explanations for this, but Rose interrupted his thoughts. "Come here," she said. "Take the baby's legs."

Martin looked down at Clover. "What should I do with them?"

"Just hold onto them."

Martin did as he was told. He put two fingers gently on each little ankle and held them.

"He's not made'a glass," she scolded. "Lift 'em up so I can clean his bottom!"

"Oh." Martin lifted Clover's legs a little higher now. The baby seemed to like that and cooed.

"Don't worry, he won't bite ya. Talk to him." Rose wiped the baby's butt.

Martin's nose curled at the smell. "What am I supposed to say?"

"It doesn't matter, he can't understand you."

"Then why would I talk to him?"

Rose applied baby powder and waved Martin off so she could put on a new diaper. "You haven't been around babies much, have you?"

Martin shook his head.

"Never had kids?"

"No."

Rose finished diapering the baby. She held up Clover to Martin.

"Well, then it's time you got to know one. Here."

Martin didn't move a muscle. "I don't think that's a good idea."

Rose gestured for Martin to take it. "Go on."

Martin put a hand on each of the baby's two sides and lifted him awkwardly.

"Turn him around so you can see him. Hold him from the bottom." Martin did and found himself looking into Clover's face. He and the baby eyed each other curiously.

"Why, hello there," he said with a quick glance to Rose to see if he was doing it right. She motioned for him to keep going. "My name is Martin. Martin Mancosa. It's nice to meet you."

Clover grinned, as if in response.

Martin's face lit up, taken by surprise. "Did you see that?"

Rose didn't respond, so Martin started to walk around, keeping his eyes on Clover. "It was a pretty warm day today, don't you think? I hear it's going to be a little cooler tomorrow."

Rose made sure Martin was facing the other way before she allowed a tiny smile.

Bill motioned for me to jump down off the counter. I rolled my eyes and started to walk away, but he put his hands on the backs of my shoulders and led me to the stove. At the side of the stove, the pot of cooked potatoes was cooling. They could have been mashed, fried or thrown against the wall.

"Seriously Bill, this is not a good idea."

"You can do this."

"I really can't."

"Close your eyes."

"Bill . . ."

"Close them."

"Aren't you supposed to see where you put the ingredients?"

He gave me a look and I closed my eyes.

"I want you to take a deep breath and relax."

I did, but it wasn't working. "I was more relaxed a minute go," I said.

"Take another one."

I did.

"And another."

Despite myself, I was starting to feel a bit calmer.

"Now I want you to picture someone," he said. "Best if it's someone you love. Like your mother."

"Bzzzzz," I said like a game show host. "'Wrong answer, Chuck. Try again.'"

"All right. Picture Rose."

"This is so stupid."

"Just picture her. Can you see her?"

Standing with my eyes closed, it wasn't hard to imagine that stern face.

"Okay . . ."

"See her eyes. Picture her breathing in and out. Can you see that?"

I nodded.

"Good. Start breathing along with her. The two of you together. Breathing in. Breathing out. In . . ." He was speaking now to match the rhythm of my breath. "And out."

I could see Rose so clearly, that I barely noticed when Bill took his hands off my shoulders. I don't know how long it was before he spoke again.

"When you're ready," he said, "start cooking."

It was really strange. I don't know how, but I knew that Rose liked her potatoes cooked in a skillet with mostly oil and a little butter for flavor. I felt sure she couldn't have salt, maybe because of high blood pressure. So she used rosemary, garlic powder and, strangest of all, a little bit of mayonnaise.

I said all this to Bill with my eyes shut, then I turned to look at him. "Is that right?"

Bill shrugged. "I don't know, is it?"

I went to the kitchen door and poked my head into the living room.

"Hey, Rose, you like potatoes cooked with mostly oil, a little butter, rosemary, garlic, and a little bit of mayo?"

"That's my favorite," she said. "Bill did it again!"

I let the door close and turned back to Bill. My mouth was open. I started jumping up and down. "Yes! Yes!"

It seemed like a whole world had just opened up. I ran and hugged
Bill. I knew just before I did that it was a leap of familiarity. I didn't
care. This was too exciting.

The timer dinged for the meat and Bill had to step away. It's weird,
but the moment he did I felt a sense of loss, like part of me didn't want
to let him go.

Maybell looked good as new as she came out of her bedroom. She
had long ago mastered the art of being able to shine after a shitty day.

"I'm goin' out. Don't wait up," she said, heading for the door.

The rest of us were sitting down for dinner. Bill removed the aluminum foil from the baking pan, sending a pungent smell of meat and
ketchup into the air. It hit Maybell as she reached for the knob.

She slowly walked back to eye the food.

Because Martin had eaten alone most of the last fifty years, he was
having a hard time navigating the confusing traffic of passing platters.
Rose's nurturing instinct kicked in, and she made sure he got fed.

"Chipped beef," Bill said to Maybell. "There's plenty."

She stared a long moment. From her face, you might have thought
she had reached a fork in the road of her life, unsure which direction
to take.

Finally she grabbed a plate and sat down.

I looked at Bill. He didn't show it, but I believed this was exactly
what he intended.

Bill was out back, standing in his usual spot, looking up at the
stars. I was at the back door, in my usual spot, looking at Bill.

I noticed the light go out under Maybell's door. It was the first time

I ever knew her to go to bed before eleven. I suppose even depression can lead to some healthy lifestyle choices.

Watching Bill reminded me of a time long ago when I was also mesmerized by the night sky. That fascination ended for me around the time I lost interest in things on the ground. I felt that sense of wonder again. It was less about the stars and more about the man who stood alone in the dark watching them.

"Eggs are change.

"Change is everything.

"Where we come from, everything Is.

"Here, on a planet, everything changes into something else.

"You never really know what will happen before an egg hits the grill."

—*Bill Bill, Interview at Maybell's Diner*

It felt so unfamiliar to actually be sitting down in Maybell's Diner, that I realized it had been years since I'd eaten there. I had sworn off diner food when I was twelve, going on thirteen, around the time I swore off Maybell. Up until then, I had grown used to watching her making a daily wreck of her life, with a parade of filler boyfriends. It seemed natural for her to do that because it was all I knew. But when I finally realized I was both part of that wreckage and in charge of cleaning it up, the last of the good will I had evaporated. Among the decisions I made: I would never let her feed me again.

And yet there I sat, a place setting in front of me, a bottomless cup ready to be filled, just like any other customer. I could feel some of the locals looking at me. After hearing me rail against the diner, I suppose they thought I was a hypocrite, or that Maybell had drugged me.

Actually, Maybell was itching for me to get my order mind-read. She thought Bill's cooking might whittle some of the chip off my shoulder. But I wasn't there for Maybell. I wanted to know what it would feel like for Bill to see deeply inside me, the way I'd done with Rose. I was skeptical—not about Bill, but about the possibility of finding anything in that diner I'd want to eat.

With the place packed, I had some time before my meal came. I looked at the people around me to try to guess what their orders might be. It wasn't too hard to know whose minds to read first. I eliminated anyone who had food and focused on those who'd already had their drink orders delivered. It was a good system. Most of the people I focused on were served soon after.

I would study a face and then close my eyes and picture it, breathing the way Bill had taught me. In most cases, all I got was a blank. But with four people, I knew right away, in a flash, exactly what they wanted. I could picture the plate, the eggs or whatever. And I picked up on some specifics, like how they wanted the melting butter to slide down the stack of pancakes. I wrote it all in my notebook before the orders came, just to keep myself honest. I had no idea why it worked only for those four. I made a mental note to ask Bill about it later.

Then I saw Martin taking a seat at the far end of the counter. He didn't see me, and that was fine. I wasn't in the mood for dumb small talk. Instead, I looked in his direction and closed my eyes. I flashed though the kinds of food you can get in a diner and tried to guess what he wanted. I got nothing. He was a blank slate to me.

But then, with my eyes still closed, I felt a sort of wave. Just one. I had no idea what it was. I had never been on a boat, but I imagined that's what it would feel like. The wave seemed strong enough to knock me over, and my hand reflexively held onto the counter. Right after that, with my eyes still closed, it seemed to me that Martin was sitting at the stool next to me, not at the other end of the counter. I could almost smell him. And then all at once, I knew with absolute certainty that there was something about Martin that was going to change all our lives. I didn't know what it was. But I also knew for sure that Bill knew it too. That's why he had invited Martin for dinner.

Right after that, something else happened and it was the strangest thing of all. While I was sitting there, I had a sensation that I was also someplace else. Like there was another me, maybe me at another time, and I was with her. Or maybe she was with me. Or maybe both. It helped to know that the other me was as freaked out about this strange coming together as I was. It made me less afraid.

I tried to picture where that other me was. I couldn't, and I realized why. That other me had her eyes closed. I could sense a sound, though, an engine running, like in a car. And there was something else. That other me, in that other place, in that car, felt a leg pressed up against hers. I have no idea why, but I knew for sure it was Bill she was sitting next to. And the two of them, Bill and that other me, were in the back seat. Because I had never been in a back seat with Bill, I figured this other me must be in the future.

The whole thing lasted just a few seconds before that other me vanished.

I opened my eyes and looked at Bill. I thought for sure he'd be looking at me, knowing what had just happened. But he was busy cooking. The diner seemed normal again.

I noticed Maybell and Dolene, working their asses off without a spare second for anything but delivering plates and clearing tables and getting the job done. Rose was some help, showing people to tables and delivering drinks. But the weight of that packed diner was on those other two. I had always known in the abstract that Maybell worked hard. I had no appreciation for it until then.

Dolene stopped by the grill. Bill quickly pointed to a few plates and went back to his cooking. Dolene swept them up and, as she passed by, she laid one in front of me and kept going. I remember thinking I liked it more when people were too busy to talk.

And then I looked down at my plate.

On one side were three slices of tomato, taken from the middle. These weren't pre-sliced from the refrigerated drawer. I hated pre-sliced anything. Bill used a fresh tomato. On the other side of the plate was half an avocado, also freshly sliced.

In a diner it's almost impossible to find food that's actually living. But Bill managed to cull some fresh grapes, cantaloupe, and cucumber from the garnish bin along with sliced peppers. He turned it into a medley of beautiful colors in the center of the plate. And in the center of that, because I would never eat anything that touched Maybell's grill, Bill placed one soft-boiled egg, sprinkled with salt and paprika.

It's not quite that Bill mind-read my order. There was nothing

I wanted from that place. Instead, he saw what I didn't even know myself. He looked into me and saw what I needed.

I stood up. I'm sure the noise of the diner was still there, but I couldn't hear it. I tried not to look at anyone as I made my way to the bathroom. I was grateful to find it unoccupied. I don't know what I would have done otherwise.

I closed the door behind me and locked it. I managed to sit down on the toilet and get my sweatshirt off just in time. I bunched it on my lap and buried my face in the folds to muffle the sound. And then I started crying.

I cried because someone, in my sixteen years of being alive, had finally seen me. And because being seen was more beautiful than anything I had ever known. I cried because it had never happened before and because I hadn't even known it mattered. It felt like Bill had shined a light on the cave I lived in and now I knew it was a cave. I would never be okay living there again.

I don't know how much time passed before I heard someone knocking. I lifted my head and called, "Just a minute!"

I wiped my face on my sweatshirt and put it back on. I didn't want to look in the mirror. I opened the door and walked right past a woman and her two kids waiting to get in. I went straight for the entrance, keeping my head down. And then I was outside.

I walked quickly by the line of people waiting to get in and then through the crowded parking lot. On the main road, cars were backed up on both sides. I started walking toward school. I don't know why. I guess I had nowhere else to go.

Somewhere in my awareness I noticed a guy and a girl, a few years older than me, sitting in a red Camaro, stuck in that traffic. In the back of my mind it registered that they seemed a little young to be interested in a mind-reading grill cook. And then I stopped thinking about them.

K atie just wanted to take a last look at the diner before they left town. She wasn't planning to go inside.

It was hard to believe that Peter was in there, not a hundred feet away. Probably wearing that same white outfit and apron, cooking for strangers. He never once cooked for her, except maybe to make her some toast in the morning. Now he was some kind of cooking star. Did she ever really know the guy?

Katie had grown up in a bland suburb of Phoenix. Her father lived at the house, even though he and her mother couldn't stand each other. It cost too much to move out and he said he'd be damned if he'd pay for two houses. He had a good job in fleet sales for one of the big rent-a-car companies. But he was unhappy at home and took to seeing other women, occasionally staying out all night. He also took to drinking.

One night he came home drunk. Katie was in her PJs watching TV, about thirteen at the time. The third button from the top had come off and she had meant to sew it on, but kept forgetting. Her father said he just wanted to see them. His body was heavy against her and she couldn't push him off. He was her father, he said. Everything in that house belonged to him and he just wanted to have a look. But he didn't just look. His fingers squeezed her nipple hard, and she could feel him growing against her leg. She looked him right in the eye and that disarmed him a bit. She was able to push out from under him and ran out the patio door. If he came after her, she'd jump the wall and start screaming for the police. But he didn't. The fucker actually picked up the remote and started watching TV.

That night changed everything for her. Katie started staying out late, going further from the house each night. Eventually she fell in with some kids who introduced her to the wonderful world of hard drugs. The kind of drugs that made every muscle in her body feel relaxed, that seemed to know her personally and wrapped her up in a cozy, warm cocoon.

At seventeen, about half a year from graduating, she was at a party in Tucson where she saw Peter for the first time. The way he held his beer, it was like he could take it or leave it. Same with the party. He wasn't trying to get anything from the world. He could take or leave that too. From that first moment, Katie was in love.

He could be harsh with others. She'd seen him slap Cyril around when they thought she wasn't there. Once, when someone tried to rip him off, Peter pulled out a gun and held it like he'd been holding guns his whole life. But Peter was always soft with Katie. The way his hand stroked her face, the loving way he held himself inside her, not rushing like every other guy. In a world that felt cold and hostile, Peter was her home.

On Main Street, Cyril had reached the point where he either had to turn in to the parking lot or drive past. That morning, Katie had barely said a word to him. Just, "Drive to the diner." Well, he drove there.

"Whatta you wanna do, Katie?"

She just stared at the diner. It suddenly hit her that, if they left now, she'd never see Peter again, not for the rest of her life. Cars started to honk behind them.

"Katie . . .?"

Katie opened the passenger door. "Do whatever the fuck you want!" She got out, slamming the door behind her. She started walking back down the main road, the way they came.

More cars honked. Cyril drove forward, pulling over to the right shoulder. It took him five minutes before he could turn around. And then he was stuck in the line of traffic going the other way. By the time he reached Katie she was already half a mile down the road.

He rolled down the window. "What are you doing?"

"I'm tired, Cyril. I'm going back to the motel."

"We checked out."

"Well, check back in! I didn't sleep last night."

Cyril took a breath. All he wanted was to get the hell out of that town and start putting miles between himself and Peter. Well, maybe she just needed some sleep. He did too. Her pacing around had kept him up most of the night. He supposed he could figure out some excuse at the motel. Tell them his girlfriend was sick. Checkout time wasn't supposed to be 'til eleven anyway. If they just napped a couple of hours, maybe he wouldn't have to pay for another night.

"Get in," he said.

She closed the door behind her and kept her eyes on the road. They drove in silence.

Martin entered from the kitchen. He was dressed in kitchen whites that were too big and made him look like a teenager with gray hair. Two snaps in the shirt were undone because he couldn't get them to close.

He found Bill at the grill. "I really don't see the point of this."

Bill looked at Martin and smiled. "You look great. Was that the only size?"

Maybell came bounding over. "What the hell is going on?"

Martin opened his palms in a gesture of innocence. He found Maybell pretty intimidating. "This wasn't my idea."

"Of course it wasn't." She looked at Bill pointedly.

Bill said simply, "We need more help."

"Oh, and that's for you to say? You got any other ideas while you're at it? Health insurance and pension maybe? Profit sharing? I know— why don't we change the name to Bill's Diner?!"

She turned from Bill to Martin. She couldn't help but think he looked like the kind of lost dog you didn't want to leave outside. She let out a sigh. "Just don't break anything. Rose!"

Maybell led Martin over to Rose, who was handing out change at the register.

"Show Martin about bussin' dishes."

Maybell went off to pour coffee. Rose looked Martin up and down. Her gaze made him uncomfortable, and she was sorry about that. Years of working in the library had given her an intimidating glare that was hard to shake off. She actually thought he looked kind of cute. But he'd missed two snaps, and she reached to correct that. I don't know why it is that mothers, after having indisputable control over what their babies wear, feel they have license to dress the rest of us.

"There. Now you look presentable."

Rose tried to remember the last time she had helped a man get dressed. It was Jessie for sure. In the hospital. How many times did she get him in and out of his pajamas when he couldn't do that for himself? He'd probably be about Martin's age if he had lived. The realization made Rose suddenly self-conscious.

She pointed to a dish bin under the counter. "All you gotta do is bus the dirty bin to the kitchen and bring clean dishes back."

Martin nodded and let out a sigh. "I don't know why I'm doing this. Working in a diner is not a life experience I was looking for."

Rose chuckled. "Me neither. I'd say half my life experiences were like that."

Martin looked at the heavy dish bin and frowned.

"You'll do fine," Rose said.

Martin nodded and hefted it up, struggling to find his balance. As he started for the kitchen, Rose was seized by an overwhelming impulse to pinch his buns. She managed to stop herself just in time, and Martin disappeared in the kitchen. But she smiled that such a thought could enter her mind at her age.

As Bill lifted his spatula, the din of a hundred thoughts, a hundred yearnings, disappointments, wants unfilled, aspirations, losses, gratitudes, tragedies—the whole of a diner-full of lives—washed over him. He was caught up with them, concerned for them, connected to them, filled by them. He was one with their stories and one with them.

It was so beautiful, so compelling, so sad and joyful that, in that moment and in the moments that came after, Bill began to lose track of his own story and what had brought him there.

The evening was strange exactly because it was so normal. Sonny Boy helped set the table, just like I'd seen kids do on TV. And he was talking with Bill the way normal people talk, about dumb, normal stuff. It was like this weird kid I knew for thirteen years had suddenly become a person.

Rose had arrived with a gift for Clover who, I'm embarrassed to tell you, had never received a real present before that night. It took some time to introduce him to the idea of unwrapping. If you had a camera in Maybell's house, like on a TV show, you would have thought Rose was the grandmother. Martin, who followed her directions and collected the discarded paper, would have played the grandfather.

Bill would have been harder to cast. He was too young for the father and, at around twenty-five, too old for the big brother. Earlier, when we stopped at the P&Q to shop for dinner, Bill had me deciding the meal for everyone. There I was, standing in the produce section, eyes closed, trying to read minds. I couldn't tell if I got it right, but Bill was reassuring. I guess he could have played the friendly guidance counselor.

Maybell was the other cast member who was out of place. Whatever nurturing role a mom usually has on a TV show was completely beyond her. She stayed in her room with the door closed until Bill announced dinner, then she plodded out to join us in a robe over loose clothes. I suppose if this was a TV show, Maybell would have been the whacky alcoholic mom.

My role was a total cliché: the rebellious teenage girl. You could practically hear the laugh track when I spoke, though I wasn't saying much that night. The meal from the diner was still at work in me, burrowing its way down. I thought this must be what it was like to have something foreign, like a baby, growing inside you. Whatever it was—a potential, an unraveling—it was set in motion by Bill.

I'm glad there were no TV cameras that night. They would have shown me staring at him all through dinner.

That meal was the most normal eaten in that house. There was talking, laughing, passing food—things every family does and that ours never had. In the middle of all this was Bill. Listening to us. Curious. I guess Bill didn't need to play a role in this show. He was writing it.

Rose had been standing motionless inside her living room from the moment she got back. After the din of Maybell's house, Rose's had never felt so empty, except right after Jessie died. The minutes ticked by and seemed as endless as her home seemed quiet. It felt like someone had sucked all the air out and, as in outer space, there was nothing to carry the sound. She wondered how she ever came to get used to that silence.

She had married Jessie while she was still at community college, which meant she had never experienced living alone until after he died. She was forty-three when he did. It was more than a year after his death before she even thought of her position as a single woman. She began to realize it meant she was no longer part of the world. No longer part of anything, really. With her son out of the country, she had no more people. She felt like an outcast who just happened to be living in the same house and the same town where she lived before her exile.

Sometimes she would notice a man her own age who she knew to be single. It would happen at the diner or maybe the supermarket. It wasn't that Rose was thinking of marrying again or even dating. What struck her was that none of these men ever seemed to notice her. For them, for the world, Rose had become invisible. She wondered why. She was still a person inside that middle-aged body. But gradually she accepted it, like she accepted the silence in her home, as the way things were, something she could live with if she didn't think about it.

Now that silence was closing in on her, threatening to crush her. That's when she thought about the man with those sad eyes and that frail manner, living alone himself in a world for which he was no match. A world that had forgotten him, as it had forgotten her. She could picture his tender hands and his cute little buns hiding under those kitchen whites.

She realized then why her house felt unbearable. He wasn't in it.

As Rose started to get ready for bed, she felt she could accept the silence now, knowing she would see Martin tomorrow at the diner.

Martin had been sitting in his '87 Cutlass for twenty minutes. His motel door was just ten feet away, yet it could have been ten miles. When exertion caught up with him, he would always feel it in his legs. Those took the longest to come back.

He was waiting now and knew he had to be patient.

He had tried to get Bill to talk with him that night. Bill seemed to think the timing had to be right. But that was the problem that was becoming clear to Martin as he sat there watching the minutes tick off on his car's analog clock.

Time was running out.

Katie stood by the sink and regretted not thinking this through. When she locked herself in the bathroom, it hadn't occurred to her to bring her drugs from the bag. She and Cyril were having a day-long fight. As tired as she was that morning, she couldn't fall asleep. She didn't want to go back to the diner, but she also wouldn't leave town. And Cyril was fuming about paying for another night at the motel.

Their fighting had peaked an hour before, after which she slammed the bathroom door and locked herself inside. No way she was going to give up that door now. It was the one advantage she had in this whole world, the only thing that kept Cyril out of her face.

Just one pill would have made that bathroom tolerable.

On the other side, Cyril was still trying to talk her out. "Peter's the asshole! Not me!" He banged on the door.

Christ, he thought. Hadn't he stood by her? Gone to the freakin' 7-Eleven five times a day for her?

"Katie!"

"Leave me alone, Cyril!"

Earlier he'd taken her to the mall for lunch, hoping something kind of normal might get her mind off Peter. Sure, Peter didn't want her anymore. That sucks, but get over it.

Cyril did everything right. He drove Katie. Paid for gas and food. And, by the way, two nights in a motel and no sex?! How many guys would put up with that? What more did she want from him?

It was Peter who wrecked everything. And after agreeing that Katie was Cyril's. Even now, that asshole could find a way to ruin Cyril's life.

He heard Katie crying through the door. And that's when it dawned on him. He wondered why he hadn't realized this before. Katie wasn't crying because of him. It was because of Peter. It was Peter who hurt her, not Cyril.

The feeling came back, the one Cyril had had in the car yesterday. Peter had hurt his girl. Now Cyril wanted to protect her.

He went to the pile of clothes on the chair and started to sift through them. Somewhere near the bottom he found his jacket. But the pocket was empty. No gun.

He went through all the clothes twice. Looked on the chair, under it, around the whole room. It wasn't there.

Then he remembered that, earlier in the food court, the jacket had slipped off his chair. The gun must have fallen out while it was on the floor. When he put the jacket back on, he had forgotten there was supposed to be something heavy in the pocket.

He thought the gun must be sitting on the floor of the food court right now. He checked the clock: 11:38. The mall was probably closed. And someone would have found it anyway. Maybe a janitor. He knew it wasn't registered. He'd never get it back.

Screw it, he thought. There'd be too many people around anyway. It was stupid to use a gun. He'd find some other way to take out that asshole. He threw the pile of clothes back onto the chair. That's when he caught site of himself in the mirror.

There he was, plain old Cyril. Cyril who no one paid attention to, who would never amount to anything. Cyril was going to protect beautiful Katie. He stood up a little straighter. He felt like a hero in a movie.

I was standing by the back door again. Sonny Boy and Maybell were in their rooms. Clover was down in his crib. I don't know how long I was there before I opened the door and went outside. I wasn't intending to do that. I didn't even realize I had, until I felt the night air on my face. I walked over to where Bill was looking up at the stars. I told myself I wanted to see what he was seeing. But that wasn't the truth. I wanted to be next to him.

I'm sure he knew I was there, but he didn't look at me. We stood in silence for a long time, the two of us looking up.

Slowly, a wave of discomfort came over me, growing stronger fast. The quiet between us started to seem unnatural, as if the only point of two people being near each other was to talk. That surprised me because I hated pointless chitchat. Yet there I was, crushed by the weight of silence, pain spreading through every muscle in my body like an infection. I thought I would have to run into the house.

Then the pain started to ease on its own. Gradually, in its place, there was a stillness, and in that stillness I began to feel a sense of peace. It was penetrating, like something I had been aching for without even knowing. Bill was there with me, but that didn't matter anymore. I felt completely alone under the stars.

They looked remote and cold, as always. But soon they started to seem more alive, less like distant points of light. The more I stared, the less distant they seemed. Even the idea of distance started to seem kind of quaint. Sure, there was space between me and the stars, but I could also see that there wasn't. I could see that in a way we were all part of one thing. It just happened to be a very big thing. And even that, the idea of big, started to seem outdated. The separation between us, me and the stars, didn't seem to matter in that moment.

As the feeling of distance started to evaporate, I felt a calm that I had never known in my life, before or since. I finally understood why Bill came out there every night. I felt certain he had this same feeling and it was why he came. In fact, I figured I was only able to feel this because of some sort of osmosis, being close to Bill. I think it's the reason he said nothing to me, so that I could experience this.

It occurred to me then that, unlike anyone I had ever known, Bill was completely his own person. The way he cooked and brought people together and yet didn't quite belong with anyone. Everything about him was uniquely Bill.

When I realized that, I could see for the first time that the same wasn't true for me. Up until that moment, I really thought I was my own person. But the truth was that my room, my clothes, my hair, my attitude, all of it was something I had put on, like a costume. I thought of all the people I had judged in my life: for the way they spoke and dressed, for the things they said and didn't say, for not really being themselves. And now I saw that I was just like them. The only real difference was that their costumes were designer-made to help them blend in. Mine was homemade to make me stand out.

You might think seeing this would have upset me. But, if anything, I felt relief. I didn't know until just then how heavy my costume had become or what a burden it was to wear. I began to wonder, with a sense of excitement, who I was without it.

Bill had seen through it. When he taught me to mind-read Rose, when he made me that lunch at the diner, it was because he could see me. He knew who I was despite it, not because of it.

The air grew still between us and I began to notice the sound of his breathing. A realization started to press down on me like gravity. I didn't want to see it. I knew it would change things I wasn't ready to change. But it kept pressing, so I finally gave into it and turned to look at Bill.

There was no separation between Bill and the stars or between Bill and anything. He was, in his own way, naked. There was nothing about him that was meant to hide or protect himself. It was the most beautiful thing I had ever seen in a human being.

I had to resist the urge to take his hand in mine. And to put my lips on his.

I had lived nearly seventeen years in a world that made no sense. And now, standing next to Bill, all the pieces fit together like they always belonged.

I wasn't who I thought I was. I was someone who could love.

I turned back to look at the stars. But I wasn't seeing them anymore. My mind was fixed on Bill.

B y eight that morning, the line of cars waiting to park at Maybell's was backed up to the light on Mesa Verde. Chief Munt stationed a Deputy at the light so people leaving their homes could get to work. But the going was slow, and the residents were honking to get by.

The Deputy got on his walkie: "Jesus Christ, Chief, it's midtown Manhattan here!"

"Watch your language, son," Munt radioed back. "We've got visitors."

The Chief had made an arrangement with the Century 21 across the street to take runoff from Maybell's parking lot. It wasn't the people who came to town that concerned him. It was the people who seemed determined to stay. Emma's already had three new RVs and the eight on Route 32 was half full. His deputies took to calling them pilgrims, even though Munt told them not to. He didn't mind strangers so much. He just didn't like the unexpected.

For himself, he was agnostic about Bill. His own taste in breakfast was pretty ordinary, so when Maybell brought him a plate with scrambled eggs, home fries and buttered white toast, it didn't seem like much of a stretch to guess that order. Though it did taste really fine.

Most people, he thought, had a hunger for something that was outside the normal routine of day-to-day life. He supposed Bill fed that hunger. He didn't particularly care if Bill was legitimate, as long as everyone stayed safe.

When he stopped traffic on Main Street to wave pedestrians across from the Century 21, he didn't give a thought to the young man in the jacket walking among them. Once the group was across the street, the Chief waved the cars forward and went back to keeping an eye on traffic.

Cyril leaned down, pretending to tie his shoe and let the others get on line before him. He needed a moment to figure out what to do.

He had eaten two complimentary muffins at the motel. No way he was going to pay for breakfast here and put money in Peter's pocket. Besides, if he walked in the front door, Peter might see him. When Cyril was sure the police chief was looking the other way, he slipped between some cars and walked around to the back of the diner.

With the diner filling up, there was less room for a baby in a bubble walker. I wouldn't have brought Clover, but a diner was still better for him than a high school. Besides, Maybell carved out a spot between the last booth and the bathroom, where Clover could bounce around clear from the foot traffic. Locals who knew him would always say hi, so he never wanted for company.

I pushed my way up the line and inside. Maybell was on the other side of the diner and too busy to notice me. Rose was finally experiencing the hell of being a waitress. She held a tray full of drink orders and laid them at the double table.

A boy at the table next to her asked, "Can I have another soda?"

"Soon as I grow a third hand," Rose snapped.

After I placed Clover in his walker, I looked over at Bill. He was able to work both very fast and deliberately, so that he seemed to be taking his time. I imagined if you were watching a great painter, it would look much the same.

As I just stood there, I felt a disturbing feeling in my belly. It was a pang. Of course I knew what it was. I knew it the night before after me and Bill came inside from the backyard. He went off to his cot in Sonny Boy's room, and I got ready for bed.

I was in the bathroom brushing my teeth when I stopped to look in the mirror. I noticed my robe was open just a bit, and I could see the tops of my breasts. When your mom uses cleavage as a weapon of mass destruction, you come to hate it on general principle. I had decided not to accept my own, much the way a rich man might refuse to acknowledge his bastard son.

But as I looked at it then, it started to seem intriguing. I gently stroked the skin and felt a tingle run down my legs. I got so light-headed I had to sit on the toilet. The feelings were coming at a rapid clip, too fast for me to make sense of them. But standing out among them: it became at once painful and wonderful to know that Bill would be sleeping ten feet from my bed.

All my life I had assumed that sexuality had passed me by. I was glad about that. Sexuality was a ruinous force that destroyed everyone in its path. Maybell was lost to it. So were the men who pursued her. It's what had brought me, Sonny Boy, and Clover into this world, to no good end as far as I could tell.

But as I sat in the bathroom, I could see it hadn't missed me at all. It had simply been waiting for the time when it would awaken. And that time was upon me. Not in a general way, like it is with guys. Their desire could be attached to anyone. Mine belonged only to Bill.

I watched him as he cleared half a dozen meals off the grill in the time it takes someone to open a book. It didn't bother me at all that he was older. Maybe he had eight or nine years on me. It could have been a hundred, for all I cared. I was born old. If you were to put our two internal ages side by side, I would have come out ahead. But something else was bothering me. A question. Would Bill ever feel that same pang for me?

As I watched him, I began to sense that I wasn't the only one. Other women at the diner, some single and some not, had one eye on Bill. I could understand why. He was the star attraction of Hadley. A celebrity, really. It hit me that half the women in Hadley must have had Bill on their radar.

I remembered a look on Dolene's face a few days back and realized in hindsight that she kind of liked Bill. I was relieved to see she was too busy to be thinking of him now. But still, there was interest.

All my life I hated the way women primp themselves to be attractive. From our first doll, we are taught to prepare for a lifetime of contortion in order to get a man. Why women agreed to this supplicating role, I do not know. But in doing so, they created a field of competition that others had to join or else be left behind.

I had long sworn off vying in this arena because I was lucky enough to not want men. But, as I looked around the diner now, I realized a fairly peaceful chapter in my life had suddenly ended before I even knew it existed. I was now in competition for a guy. A new, shitty chapter had just begun.

Bill was too busy to notice me or any other woman there. But I was going to have to find some way to get him to see me, and not just as a housemate or some girl sitting on the kitchen counter. If I didn't, this pang in my gut was going to turn to pain, and that pain was going to become unbearable. I hated that after all this time I was now entering Maybell's world. I hated her world. But this was Bill, and if I wanted him I would have to take a giant step inside it.

I swallowed my revulsion and left the diner.

Around that time, Cyril had found the back door and looked inside the kitchen.

There was some kid washing dishes, facing away from the door, oblivious to everything with his headphones blaring. An old man brought in a tub of dirty dishes and laid them next to the kid. Whenever Cyril saw an old man doing a menial job he promised himself to never wind up like that. Somewhere in his mind he made a note to finish his GED and start saving for community college.

With the kid facing the other way, the old man leaned on a table for support. The guy seemed out of breath. He stood upright suddenly when an old woman walked in and started talking to him. The old man listened to her and then there was a pause. The old lady looked around to make sure no one was able to see them. Cyril had to duck back out a moment. He got ready to tear ass out of there. But hearing nothing, he slowly leaned forward until he could take a peek inside. The old lady was kissing the old man. So gross! The kid washing dishes had no idea.

Cyril hoped he died long before he reached that age.

The old lady finished kissing the geezer, gave him a smile, then went back out to the diner. The old man was facing the other way, so Cyril couldn't see his face. But from the way the guy just stood there, Cyril thought he must be really disgusted. Then the old guy took an empty bin and went back out into the diner.

Cyril looked around the kitchen until he saw something that would work. He stepped quietly inside, careful to keep behind the dishwasher. On the prep table he found a paring knife. The blade was about four inches long.

And it was sharp.

I was supposed to be in school by now. I'd much rather have been there than where I was standing. It was outside Brenner's Shoes. I hadn't looked in that window since I discovered Doc Martins on Zappos.com. But there I was, checking out women's shoes designed to make men attracted and walking all but impossible. I would have thought men would find a woman more appealing if she was able to make her way across the street.

The shoe store wasn't open yet, but Frieda's Salon was. In the last few years, I had only gone inside when I had to deal with Maybell. But still, every single time, Frieda moaned about how she'd love to get her hands on me. I was not shy about telling her what she could do with her hands.

Now as I looked in the window, I could see the faint reflection of my short, unruly hair. I cut it that way on purpose to keep guys away.

Frieda was inside having her coffee. She must have wondered what the hell I was doing at her window.

I forced myself to walk inside. Lord, how times change.

Maybell had so many emotional crutches, it was hard to say exactly which one she was most addicted to. Sex in general, men in particular,

Oren in extreme particular, self-pity, drama, titillation, or just a bunch of stupid ideas about what she thought her life should be like. But there was one constant: every time Oren got on his Harley and rode away from her house, even that very first time when Maybell was pregnant with me, she would always go out and get herself laid. At this she was infallible.

Until Bill's chipped beef.

That beef changed the chemical makeup of Maybell's psyche. She didn't go out looking for a guy that night, or the next night. She didn't seem to want to.

For two days at the diner, Maybell had been in a kind of fog. She waited on tables, cleared dishes. She was able to operate the cash register. But to anyone who knew her, it was like fifty percent of Maybell was still in bed.

They say when alcoholics give up booze, they experience a kind of flatness to life. Maybell had gone two days without men and she was roadkill.

Dolene met up with her behind the counter.

"May, honey, you feeling okay?"

Maybell was slow in responding.

"Yeah, I'm fine."

Maybell went on working like a prisoner in Siberia who'd finally gotten used to the cold.

Then around ten or so, with the crowd showing no sign of thinning, Marguerite pushed her way inside the diner and found Maybell. It was like the clouds parted and Maybell came back to life.

"Marguerite! Where the hell you been? I've been calling you for days! You would not believe what I've been through!"

They hugged. Marguerite looked around the diner in wonder. "Is this all from Harold's article?"

"Can you believe it?"

"There's a line practically to the road!"

Maybell led Marguerite to a slightly quieter part of the diner. "Oh, my Lord, I've got so much to tell you!"

"I got something to tell you too," Marguerite said.

They hesitated, not sure who should go first. Or rather, that's what Maybell thought was going on. Marguerite was giving her a funny face and scratching her cheek with her left hand.

"What's the matter with you," Maybell asked. "You look like the cat that swallowed—Holy goddam *shit*!" Maybell saw the wedding ring on Marguerite's finger. "You shittin' me??!"

Marguerite shook her head and smiled.

"Oh, my damn! Oh, my goddam! You're married?"

Marguerite nodded.

Maybell gave her a tight squeeze, then looked at her again. "When?"

"Two days ago! We just got back from Vegas."

"Vegas?! Lord, I can't believe you! Why the hell didn't you tell me?! I would'a stood by you! Who did you marry?"

There was just a moment of hesitation before Marguerite turned back toward the entrance. The lucky man was a little slow coming forward, afraid to meet Maybell's eye. Wayne had a sheepish look on his face as he stepped up to Marguerite. Marguerite took his hand. It was the first time the two of them allowed a PDA in front of Maybell. Wayne had an identical wedding ring.

"Hey, May . . . ," he said uneasily to the mother of his only son, a boy he had yet to meet.

"Wayne?" Maybell said softly.

Marguerite knew Maybell as well as anyone and figured this was going to be a gut-punch. She had thought about telling her best friend sooner, but Maybell had a funny way of wanting what she couldn't have. The combination of Wayne being unavailable and desired by someone else would make him way too tempting. Rather than put both her friendship and her romance on the line, Marguerite opted to keep herself and Wayne under the radar. At least until she got a ring on his finger. She figured even Maybell wouldn't cross that line. But the secrecy, she knew, would have a price. And the bill was coming due now.

I realize I have to put Maybell on pause for a moment because I haven't told you what was going on with Bill, and that's the important part right now. At the start of the day, Bill had loaded up the shelf above the grill with loaves of bread, as per usual. But today's crowd was leaning heavily on whole wheat and Bill was just about out. Plus, he could feel a lot of desire for wheat bread in that line outside.

Under normal circumstances, Bill would have been way ahead of the wheat situation. But that morning he had a lot on his mind. There was Radd, for one, who sat at the counter fretting over when to start collecting Social Security. Bill hadn't thought much about retirement planning before, but as Radd went on about inflation and nest eggs and rising insurance rates, Bill had to admit it was all very concerning. Making ends meet through old age now rose up in Bill's mind as one of life's big issues.

Then there was Mrs. Reese from the Century 21 across the street. She was going to the dentist that afternoon to get a crown and came to the diner for a meal before the big event. All that talk about dentists and twinges had gotten Bill wondering about some pain he was starting to feel in his own mouth, along the bottom left side, toward the back. He had heard of dental work before he rose up off that gurney in Phoenix Memorial. It was only dawning on him now the amount of responsibility he had taken on, along with a human body. What other maintenance issues were going to crop up? When Mrs. Reese spelled out the cost of a crown and a possible root canal, Bill got to wondering if, like Harley, he should be asking Maybell for a raise.

All that is to say that the whole wheat took Bill by surprise. He would have asked Martin to go get more from the back, but Dolene tapped Martin to help bus tables 2 and 5. So Bill cleared the grill for a moment and went into the kitchen.

Because the kitchen was so small, Maybell kept the bread rack just outside the back door. Coincidentally, that rack allowed Cyril a pretty good hiding spot, while he waited for his chance to sink that paring knife into Bill.

That chance was coming now.

Okay, now I can take Maybell off pause.

Marguerite was sensing a shift in Maybell's mood. Trying to avoid an uncomfortable moment for the three of them, she opted to change the subject.

"I almost forgot! We're taking over the bowling alley tonight."

Marguerite turned and shouted to the rest of the diner. "Hey, everybody!"

Marguerite whistled to quiet the place down. "There's gonna be a wedding party tonight over at Dave's Bowl! Lanes are on me and Wayne!"

Marguerite held up her ring finger like a king raising his sword in victory. The place erupted in cheers; both from locals and visitors. I guess that's just the generic response when you hear about a wedding. Never mind there's a fifty percent chance it won't last and a near certainty it will be miserable. People are lost to the power of denial.

But that denial was what saved Bill.

He was just within Cyril's striking range, when the ruckus came from inside. Bill quickly grabbed four loaves and went back in the diner. Because of the sudden noise, Cyril hesitated and missed his chance to end Bill's life. And, with Bill gone, he didn't imagine there'd be another one coming anytime soon. Plus, Katie was probably awake by now and wondering where he was. So Cyril decided to put his plan on hold and go back to the motel.

Inside, locals came around to congratulate Marguerite and Wayne. Maybell looked at Wayne, who had never seemed more handsome and eligible and prince-like. It wasn't that she wanted a future with Wayne; they had little in common and bland sexual chemistry. For sure, she wanted her best friend to be happy. But Maybell had a jukebox inside her head, and this news set off her oldest and meanest song. Its familiar refrain hammered at her over and over, louder and more convincing than ever before: "Life has passed you by."

Marguerite saw her friend looking lost and leaned in. "Hey, hon, why don't you bring Oren?"

Maybell gave her a forced smile.

Martin sat on his bed and felt himself sinking. Each day he found that staying around Bill, hoping to learn something, was taking a larger toll.

When Bill invited him for dinner that first time, Martin felt that his long search was finally over. But the whole night, Bill was evasive and that hostile woman, Rose, kept glaring at him.

The next day, when Bill suggested he work at the diner, Martin almost laughed. But then he got to thinking about *The Karate Kid* and how Mr. Miyagi would teach martial arts through menial tasks. Martin thought maybe Bill was offering to be his Miyagi. So he changed into kitchen whites and bussed dishes, thinking he might find some wisdom at the bottom of that greasy dish bin. But all he found was back pain and nostalgia for his comfortable, wood-paneled office.

Then came that second night at Maybell's house, and his world flipped on its edge.

The gathering was a little less alien and everyone a little more relaxed. During dinner, while Rose was feeding the baby, Clover made a face and a snorting sound that cracked everyone up. Martin too. He was laughing with complete abandon when it occurred to him that he couldn't remember the last time he'd done that. He wasn't sure if he ever had. Being unguarded for that moment showed him how guarded he always was. A feeling of queasiness began to rise up from deep inside. He wanted desperately to squash it down. Luckily, he was able to forget it in the conversation.

After dinner, Sonny Boy was alone on the couch, back to his game. Martin sat down to watch. He had heard so much about video games. He wanted to finally see what all the fuss was about. The game, "Call Of Duty: Black Ops," was a wonder to behold. But Martin was more struck by watching Sonny Boy play it. The boy's focus was absolute, as if he were alone in the room.

It dawned on Martin that he could have been watching himself at that age. For Martin, back then, it was books. As a boy, he had hundreds of them lining the walls of his room. Each book contained a world that Martin preferred to his own. It's not that he had a particularly bad childhood. In fact, he remembered almost nothing of it. But, like Sonny Boy, he found solace in escape.

That's when the queasiness came back. Only now it was stronger. It was nausea. Martin felt he had somehow cracked open a door to a dark place deep inside himself. And through that crack came a dank and fetid smell. In some small part of his mind that wasn't flailing in panic, Martin knew that he had hoped to die with that door sealed shut.

He stood upright, made some excuse about getting to bed early and walked out. He didn't even look back at Bill.

The next day at the diner he was glad for the grueling work to distract him. When Rose cornered him for a kiss, he could barely speak. He was in survival mode.

Now, as he was sitting on his bed at the motel, Martin felt like he was at the bottom of a deep, dark well. Fear was all around him, and it seemed that if he were to move, even a little, he would fall off a ledge and into an abyss that would have no end.

Martin imagined a small pool of light at the top of that well. And standing in that light was Bill, looking down at him. Bill wasn't reaching to rescue him, but he wasn't walking away either.

As they were leaving the diner that day, Bill had suggested that Martin come out to Dave's Bowl. And because Bill was the only light in his world, Martin forced himself to get up off his bed, pick up his keys, and head out to a wedding party.

I yelled through my bedroom door for Maybell, Sonny Boy, and

Bill to go without me. I had spent half my life communicating through that door, so it seemed only natural to do it now.

I was the first to get home that day, and I stayed in my locked room, which meant none of them had seen what I had turned into. My new shoes were a light blue. I didn't like that color, in fact I disliked it, but they were the only ones in the store that remotely fit. I owned one skirt in this world, leftover from middle-school graduation. It was plain, but still fit. Underneath I wore simple black tights because no man, not even Bill, could get me to expose my bare legs. Before Maybell came home, I snatched a top from her closet that was relatively unsleazy and didn't look too bad on me. It had a lot of red in it, with fake alabaster buttons. It didn't exactly reveal cleavage, but didn't entirely hide it.

As for my hair, I let Frieda have at it. Though she declared it mission impossible, she seemed pleased when it was done and said it reminded her of Mia Farrow, whoever that was.

My plan was to reveal my new look to Bill in a way that would have maximum impact. Sitting around the living room and just saying "Hey" didn't seem like the way to go. My plan was to wait until he was alone in the kitchen. I didn't know exactly what I hoped for. There are plenty of movies where the girl walks in the room and the guy looks up and suddenly realizes she's *it* for him. But I usually fast forward through those parts. I just knew I wanted Bill to feel about me the way I felt about him. Changing how I looked was supposed give me some control over that. But I was starting to sense how tenuous that control actually was.

It was Maybell who killed my plans. I heard her through the door announcing we were going out to the bowling alley for Marguerite's wedding party. After all that work I wasn't going to just pile into the back of Maybell's truck and take a chance on Bill missing the whole point. So I yelled back through the door that I'd meet them there.

I knew that if I wore the shoes outside the house, there'd be no returning them. If their effect was lost on Bill, they would sit in my closet for years, gathering dust, reminding me of how miserably I had failed. For the first time in my life, I appreciated Maybell's power over men, as destructive as it was in her hands.

After I heard the truck pull out, I unbolted my door and hobbled into the living room. The heels weren't high, at least that's what the clerk had told me. She called them a medium heel. Whoever made those shoes seemed to think that women had three toes and not five. I had practiced walking for the last hour in my room and still couldn't get my knees and my ankles to work together.

The babysitter was already planted deep into the sofa with a bowl of popcorn and a liter of soda. She was two years younger than me, but from the way she reacted to my outfit I knew she recognized me. Tomorrow she'd tell her friends about the freaky loner girl playing dress up. I'd be the school joke for a few days. As I hobbled to the door, I was already starting to miss the peacefulness of being ignored. The babysitter turned back to the TV. Clover was by her side, so I knew he'd at least be safe from crib death.

Outside I didn't bother with the headlight on my bike. I preferred that nobody see me riding up. I managed to get the front part of my shoes on the pedals with the heels behind, and headed off.

The only time Dave's Bowl was filled was nights like this, when someone decided it would be a good spot for a party. The rest of the time its customers were mostly old guys out to get away from their wives, or high school boys looking to get a beer without being carded.

Tonight Dave had the first three lanes closed off for dancing. That was fine by him. He made a good chunk of his money renting bowling shoes for dancers. First drink was on Marguerite and Wayne, and then everyone was on their own.

The thing that hit me every time I walked into that place was the bowling alley smell. This building went up sometime in the 1950s, and I don't think they aired it out since. The combination of alley grease, stale beer, French fries and geezer was almost enough to make me turn and leave.

I wobbled inside and held my breath, waiting for the comments. "Ooooh, Belutha looks like a girl!" "We thought you were a dude." But my new look had a surprising benefit: no one recognized me. I guessed that, with all the visitors in town, people just assumed I was a stranger.

I saw Wayne and Marguerite at the far lane, having their pictures taken. Marguerite had her arm around him like he was a prize she won at a fair. Wayne had on a game face, but I could see he was miserable being on display. When the photographer was done, Wayne made a beeline for the bar.

Maybell was already on her third beer when Wayne came for his first.

"Hey, Maybell."

"Hey, Wayne. Congratulations. You snagged yourself a winner."

"Yup, yup," Wayne said, like he was still trying to convince himself. The whole thing had started as a joke. "What if we got married? Wouldn't so and so hit the roof? We could go to Vegas. Nobody'd have a clue." Next thing he knew, she'd found this ridiculous fare on

Google Flights and what the hell, they'd gamble and if they got drunk enough to find a chapel it would be such a hoot. That's what movie stars do—right?

Wayne took a long swallow, chugging half his beer.

"Can you believe it?" he said. "Me. Married." Wayne held up his left hand, staring at the ring as if it was put on surgically while he was under anesthesia. He finished his beer and got another.

"You did it, Wayne."

"Yup." The beer was already helping him with that idea. He took a long gulp and then looked over at Maybell. "Jeez, May. I guess I just wasn't ready for the big M before. You know, when we . . ."

He put a hand on Maybell's shoulder in a gesture that was supposed to look mature. Then he noticed some friends nearby and went over to greet them.

Maybell downed the rest of her beer.

Bill had his first experience with alcohol that night. Radd brought him a beer and, with the first sip, Bill felt the impact immediately. His body became relaxed and his arms seemed a bit heavier. He studied the beer a moment, then looked at Radd.

"This is beer?"

"That's right, Billy."

"People drink this every day?"

Radd chuckled at Bill's apparent joke. "Believe it or not, some people have more than one."

Bill regretted that he had only now gotten around to trying some.

It was a night of firsts for Bill. I had been scanning the room, looking for him, when I heard a commotion on the lanes. Bill was dancing—jumping and swinging in a way that looked like he was receiving electroshock therapy. A couple of women had tried to join him, but Bill was out there on his own. He seemed completely plugged into the music, as if the music itself was his dance partner. Some of the older people had to step back to keep away from his flailing arms and flying sweat.

When the song ended, Bill stepped off the floor and met up with Radd, who had been holding Bill's beer and now handed it back. Bill was nearly halfway through it and delighted to find that drinking more actually increased its impact. There were people standing nearby, waiting for their chance to talk with him. Some were locals who wanted to shake his hand without a counter and a busy grill in the way. Some were visitors hoping that a little of Bill's mojo, whatever that was, might rub off.

Bill was experiencing another first that he didn't quite understand but later attributed to the beer. He let his guard down. People who came up to Bill were happy to give him their hand or a pat on the back or offer a hug. And Bill was delighted by all of it. He felt warmth toward them all, as if they were now friends for life. He was amazed to find his fear of people to be so unfounded.

As I watched, I noticed more than a few women eyeing Bill, some I thought with romance in mind. I'd have to find a way to get time with Bill sooner rather than later. I was trying to figure out how, when I noticed Martin Mancosa entering the alley. He looked even more out of place than I felt. He walked up close to where I was standing and looked over the room. I knew he was searching for Bill. Even more than the women there, Martin was my competition.

We both had realized it after dinner the night before. Bill was washing dishes, and Martin and I stood on each side to help, both of us hoping for some alone time with Bill that neither of us got because of the other.

I could see Martin's posture change when he spotted Bill. He grew more determined. Then he must have felt my eyes on him, because he turned to the side and saw me. When our eyes met, there was an instant recognition that we were adversaries after the same prize.

I thought: "Bring it on, old man!"

Then I heard a voice call from behind me.

"Hey, Belutha."

It was Rodney. I turned to him with annoyance. "Rodney, I told you it's never gonna happen. Why don't you take a cold shower or invest in some porn?"

He seemed totally unbothered. "Just wanted to say, you look really pretty tonight." Rodney smiled and walked away.

I stared at him a long moment. Then I remembered Martin. By the time I turned back, he was already on his way to Bill.

Maybell got to a table with chips and dips. That's what people in Hadley call a balanced meal. There was a tall man there, taking his time. After those beers, Maybell was getting to that point where any man would do. She went up behind him.

"Is that the only dipping you're looking to do tonight?"

The man she just hit on was Reverend Wrightwood, who either didn't hear her or pretended not to.

"Maybell, haven't seen you in many a Sunday."

"Oh, Lord," she said as he nodded and walked away. Before she had time to think about that, Harley came up to her.

"May—May—I want my job back."

"Harley . . ." She could smell the liquor on his breath. "You stink."

"That cook you got," he said not hearing her. "He's evil."

"Bill's not evil."

"Ya see?! That's my point! He's got ya under his spell."

"Harley, go home and sleep it off." Maybell turned to go, but he grabbed her wrist, more roughly than he realized.

"'Member you 'n me, May? You 'n me?"

Maybell jerked her hand away. "That was like fifth grade, Harley. I showed you my lulu and you showed me your dingdong."

Harley watched her walk away and mused quietly: "That was special." Then, he looked over and saw Bill. All those people, gathered around him like he was so important. He had them all hypnotized. Somebody had to right this wrong. At least that's what Harley told the police afterwards.

Across the room, Cyril was watching too. He realized something about the paring knife. Peter had probably used it before, which meant it would have his prints on it. Plus it looked just like the other knives back at the diner. The police would know it came from there. Cyril felt more and more like this was going to look like self-defense.

He hadn't told Katie he was coming here tonight. He had snuck out of the room while she was in the shower. Even more than the police, it was Katie who needed to be convinced that Cyril hadn't set out to kill Peter. He already planned what he would tell her. How Peter said awful things about her. How he threatened to carve her up with that knife. Cyril even figured out some motivation: Peter wanted both Katie and Cyril out of the way so he could continue his scam in this town. As far as Katie would know, Peter tried to kill Cyril and planned to kill her afterward. But Cyril had fought back bravely. He might even give himself a little poke with that knife to make it look more convincing and get some sympathy. He could practically feel her grateful arms around him.

But Peter wasn't making it easy. Too many people around him. There seemed to be no way Cyril was going to get him alone. He'd wait a while, see if the place cleared out some. If not, it'd have to be tomorrow. In the meantime, he decided to hit the snack table and then take a leak. The party was free, wasn't it?

Martin figured the locals had first dibs on Bill, so he patiently waited his turn. He could feel his legs starting to turn to rubber. It surprised him that he lasted as long as he did, working at the diner. His hip bones had been compromised by the disease, and in the last six months it had spread to his right femur, with early stages showing up in the left. He knew some people came to town hoping for a miracle healing from Bill. Martin didn't. Even if he believed in that, he was sure his illness was too far along for anyone to save his life.

I watched Martin in the crowd as he was waiting to talk with Bill. I didn't want to do that: be just another person standing by. Not when Bill slept in the room next to mine. I decided to wait. My toes felt like they were in a vise, and a pain shot up my calves.

I grabbed the nearest seat I could find. It was at a table overlooking the lanes. An older couple were sitting there. I'd seen them around town, but never met them before.

I was watching Bill put his arm around Martin as if helping to hold him up. I was touched by that gesture. Martin was talking to Bill, and Bill was listening intently. When Bill did that, he made you feel like there was no one else in the world. I was thinking about how great that was, when the woman spoke up.

"You're Maybell's daughter, aren't you?"

"Yeah," I said, without taking my eyes off Bill. I wasn't in the mood for small talk and figured being rude was the best way to nip this conversation in the bud.

"You look very nice tonight. Doesn't she, honey?"

The man nodded. "Very pretty."

Now I was pissed.

"You mean because I compromised my principles in order to fit into some generic standard of attractiveness?" I didn't mention I was trying to snag a guy. I thought they knew too much about me already.

The woman tilted her head a bit, trying to understand what I said. But her husband nodded, "Yeah. Because of that."

I could see he had a little grin, and I liked that. Some old coot showing signs of life was a pleasant surprise. But I needed to keep my eye on the prize and figured the pain in my legs was an okay price to pay.

I got back on my feet, but realized I had lost sight of Bill.

Bill rented a pair of bowling shoes while Martin waited nearby. When Bill rejoined him, he started to lead Martin out to the lanes. But Martin held his ground.

"Bill—I did everything you asked. I need to talk."

"It's not time yet."

"When will it be time? I think you know what's going on. I don't know how you know, but—well, time is not something I have a lot of," Martin admitted.

Bill stopped and looked at Martin. It wasn't the way most of us look at a person. It was penetrating. Martin felt at once uncomfortable and safe.

"The thing is, Martin, what you think you need and what you really need are not the same thing."

"That's just crazy. I need answers."

"Actually, you don't. You want them. And I understand. But the thing about the answers you're looking for, it doesn't matter if you know them. It's actually sort of better if you don't."

Martin tried to respond, but was too flustered. Bill smiled in the way that parents sometimes smile, knowing it's futile to talk rationally to their kids. Then he held up the shoes. "Let's bowl."

Bill turned and walked out to the lanes. Martin thought of just leaving. The bowling alley. The town. But where would he go? And how long would he have at this point? He shook his head and followed Bill.

Dolene was getting ready to try for a spare. Sonny Boy and Rose were at the desk, keeping score. Rose was halfway through her wine spritzer.

Bill handed Martin the shoes. "Here you go. Size 9½." He turned to the others. "Everyone, Martin's going to join us."

Dolene let the ball fall to her waist. "Aw right, Martin!" Sonny Boy gave a nod. In the Sonny Boy universe, that meant he was starting to like Martin.

Rose grew excited. She had been quietly scanning for Martin the whole night. The further down she got in her spritzer, the more often she craned her neck. She could have kissed Bill for bringing him over.

Martin looked lost. "I've never bowled before."

Sonny Boy added their names to the score chart as Rose took Martin's hand to lead him to the bench where he could change shoes. "What kind of American doesn't bowl?" She was such a well-practiced scold, no one could tell she was flirting.

I heard Dolene's scream across the alley. You couldn't miss it. Some people have so little to show for their lives that even the slightest success, like getting a spare, is cause for jubilation. I looked over, and it was then that I saw Bill in the same lane. He was stepping up to bowl. He looked pretty unnatural holding that heavy ball. He leaned toward Dolene as she stepped back to the desk.

"What am I supposed to do?"

"Knock down as many pins as you can."

Dolene could see he was still unsure, so she showed him how to hold the ball. She had one hand on his wrist, the other around his back, touching him in the way that women do when they want to let a man know it's time to start thinking about sex. I knew Dolene was dating the guy who worked at the Chevron mini mart, but it probably wasn't exclusive. Even if it was, Bill was a better catch.

No way I was going to let Dolene get her claws in. I wobbled over to the lane as fast as I could, given that I was wearing torture devices on my feet. Some pimply guy with a voice that sounded like it had just changed that morning held out his hand to block me. I think he was the owner's son.

"Excuse me, Miss. Can't go on the floor in those." He pointed to my shoes. "Only bowling shoes."

I would have loved to take them off, but that would have undercut the point of all the pain I'd been through. So instead I found a table nearby and waited.

I didn't know it at the time, but Maybell was sitting by herself about five tables from me, drinking her fifth beer. Marguerite plopped down next to her and gave her a hug. Her policy was always to tear off the Band-Aid quickly. She took a breath and dove in: "May, any time you ever talked about Wayne . . ."

"Oh, you got nothing you need to answer for. I mean it. I'm glad he does it for ya. He does do it for ya—right?"

It was a best-friend question. And normally Marguerite would give Maybell all the juicy details. But the Band-Aid was off. No need to add salt.

Marguerite just nodded and broached a new subject. "Hon, you gotta forget about Oren. That guy is a dream that ain't ever gonna come true. It's time you find yourself a real flesh-and-blood man."

Maybell turned to her. "You got one lyin' around?"

"Dunno," Marguerite said coyly. "Maybe I do."

Bill got a gutter ball while going for the spare. He didn't mind at all; in fact he was thrilled when Rose wrote down the number 4 in the box by his name. By now Bill had broken ground on his second beer. He noticed that beer seemed to fill the empty spaces between himself and other people, between lanes seven and six, between the bar and the ball rack. It seemed to him that the people, the music, the place were all welded together as one thing, connected by beer.

He took another swig.

"C'mon, Martin," Rose called. "You're up."

I don't think there's ever been a man who looked more unnatural in bowling shoes than Martin Mancosa. The red and beige leather stripes made it seem like someone else's feet were glued to his body. He followed Rose to the ball return, and she picked out the lightest one she could find. His fingers barely fit the holes. She led him to the front line and gestured for him to wind the ball back and then bring it forward. I knew Martin was an educated man, but he looked like a monkey trying to pilot an airplane.

Rose took a step back and Martin did something resembling a wind-up and then let the ball drop about a foot over the line. Still, that created enough forward momentum for the ball to roll on its own down the lane. After what seemed like ten minutes, it landed between the first and third pins. In slow motion, all the pins fell. The first ball Martin ever bowled in his life was a strike.

Bill, Sonny Boy, and Rose started cheering. The strike crown at the end of the lane lit up. Martin had a surprised look on his face.

Rose felt a thrill such as she hadn't experienced since she was my age. It seemed to her that her fate had lined up like those ten pins down the lane, falling right into place. She jumped to her feet, threw her arms around Martin, and kissed him on the lips without a care for who saw it.

Martin's excitement gave way to confusion. Why on earth was this small-town woman pursuing him? And how was it he was experiencing a sensation in his lower region, which had been dormant most of the last twenty-five years?

Maybell was watching all this with Marguerite. She shook her head. "Am I the last single gal in Hadley?"

Marguerite put a hand on Maybell's shoulder. "Honey, you got a keeper right under your nose and you can't even see it." Marguerite motioned to the lanes, over to Bill sitting next to Sonny Boy.

Maybell turned back to Marguerite in dumb surprise. "Bill?"

"He's not too hard on the eyes. He's great with your kids. And he sure as shit can cook."

Maybell turned back to the lane. "Bill?"

A party is like a merry-go-round. It moves around a lot, but it never goes anywhere. Alcohol is the fuel that makes it spin, but at some point it becomes the very thing that grinds it to a halt.

By about eleven o'clock, enough people had left to remove the feeling of excitement from the place. With less buzz and shouting, the music seemed inappropriately loud.

Dolene had given up on Bill even before her boyfriend showed up. Bill didn't seem interested, despite her flirtations. I think Bill just didn't understand them, which only made me like him more.

The group was only at frame seven because of Martin's balls heading down the lane at the speed of a baby crawling. So I took a chair over by the bar, where I found a half-empty beer tub with mostly melted ice. I was using it to soak my feet. The killing shoes were in the garbage nearby. Some geezer grabbed a beer from the tub and asked if my feet were lite or pale ale. I guess from my face he saw his joke didn't land and walked away. I had decided to give up on Bill for the night. I figured I'd ride home barefoot.

Back at the lane, Martin bowled a gutter ball and sat down on the bench behind the score desk. Seven frames had taken a heavy toll on his bones. Rose was a little too tipsy from wine and the excitement of romance to have paid attention before. But now things were quieter.

"Don't worry, Martin, you'll get 'em on the next one," she said marking the score. When she turned to smile at him, she noticed a film of sweat on his face. It wasn't from exertion. She realized he was in pain.

Martin gave her a forced smile, but she could see he wasn't going to be getting up for the next frame. In her excitement to feel romance again, Rose hadn't really taken a good look at the man she expected so much from. She hadn't seen him at all, really—just what she wanted to see. Well, he was there now, in full view. Rose felt ashamed for being so blind. And she wondered—selfishly, she thought—how much time they might have.

Bill had gotten up to go to the bathroom. Wayne, who was on a break from hearing dumb-ass compliments about how he'd finally "stepped up to the plate," had his eye fixed on Sonny Boy. When he sensed a pause in the game, he went over and sat down next to him.

"So you're Sonny Boy," Wayne said.

Sonny Boy looked at him and said nothing.

Wayne pressed on. "Well, my name is Wayne. And I guess, well, I don't guess, I know. . . . I'm your father."

Wayne allowed a moment for this life-changing hammer to come down on Sonny Boy's head. Wayne had anticipated this exchange so many times over the years. The boy crying. The two of them hugging. The hours they would spend catching up. If the boy was old enough, maybe they'd have a beer.

But Sonny Boy just stared at him. Wayne wondered for a moment if he might have sired an imbecile.

"I guess," Wayne went on uneasily, "there must be a lotta things you wanta know about me."

Sonny Boy considered that for a moment. "No, not really."

All the terrible smells of the bowling alley were compounded in the men's bathroom, thanks mostly to the urine.

Bill stood alone at the bank of urinals, surprised at how much his bladder could hold. He was enjoying the sense of dislocation his head felt from the rest of his body. He zipped himself, flushed, and went to the sink to wash up. Having found the bottom of two beers now, his senses were numbed. That's why he hadn't noticed he wasn't alone.

When he turned around, he was suddenly assaulted by something pressing against his face.

It was a woman's lips. Katie was kissing him, pushing him so hard he was up against the sink. She wrapped one arm around his back and the other around his neck. She rubbed her body against his and forced his mouth open with hers. Her tongue went into his mouth, and she put both her hands on his cheeks.

Bill's synapses were firing insanely. The immediacy of this kiss had taken over his existence. He barely noticed the door open and some guy saying, "Get a room you two," before leaving.

Katie paused. She put her forehead against his. This was the kind of moment you take after you've been lost in the desert and just had your first life-saving gulp of water. Katie caught her breath and allowed the sensation of relief to flood through her.

Finally she spoke. "Peter. What the fuck? What happened? How come you never called me?"

She kissed Bill again. Only this time, Bill's senses were interrupted. His head was starting to get clear of the effects of alcohol. He craned his neck back and looked at the girl embracing him. "Do we know each other?"

Katie chuckled, not wanting to allow for the possibility he might have meant that.

"Funny, Peter. Do you know how worried I was? They said you were fucking dead! Game over. And you're . . . not." She kissed him to prove to herself he was there. "Why did you leave? Why didn't you say anything? What the fuck are you doing here?"

Bill took a half step back. "How long have you known me?" he asked.

"What?"

"I mean, longer than a few weeks?"

"What the fuck are you talking about? I've known you since . . . forever."

Katie reached to embrace him, but Bill kept a space between them. He realized what was going on. He didn't know why he hadn't thought before that this could happen.

"Listen," he said, "This person you knew, Peter? I'm not him."

Katie stared at Bill now.

"This is his body. But your friend—he died."

Katie took a step back. She was too stunned to speak. Bill wasn't sure what to do. He knew there was something that people said at times like this. He tried to remember. And then it came to him.

"I'm sorry," he said.

Katie's disbelief started to give way to anger. "You're sorry??"

"For your loss."

"Fuck you Peter!" she shouted suddenly. "You fucker!"

Katie punched Bill in the mouth. His head snapped back as he hit the sink behind him. The force sent his body twisting and falling to the floor.

"After all this fucking time, that's how you break up with me?!" Katie kicked him in the ribs. Bill instinctively bent toward the kick to make a smaller target.

"You fucking chicken shit asshole!" Katie kicked and flailed, landing blow after blow. "Asshole! Fucking asshole! Fuck you, asshole!"

The barrage seemed endless, and then suddenly it stopped. Bill was stunned and the silence disoriented him. He wondered if minutes or hours had passed. How long had he been lying there?

He turned to look at the bathroom door and found it had just been seconds. Katie was standing over him.

"Fucking asshole!" she shouted, as the bottom of her boot came down hard on Bill's face, turning everything to darkness.

"Pleasure and pain give you important information, such as 'Don't put your hand in fire,' or 'Do make babies.' But they also play a huge role soon after you arrive.

"A baby can refuse to commit to its new life. It's a confusing and shocking time. Not everyone wants to stay. There's a temptation to remain detached or even leave.

"Pleasure and pain cause an intense identification with the new body that's hard to resist. They make the baby believe: 'I am this body. This body is me.'

"Once that identification happens, the commitment lasts until the body dies."

—*Bill Bill, Interview at Maybell's Diner*

The fog lifted around three thirty a.m. Everything before that seemed to be happening at a distance, as if Bill was deep inside his body and couldn't quite make it to the surface.

It was Radd who found him in the bathroom. Even semi-conscious, Bill recognized the voice.

"Damn, Bill, hold tight. I'll go get . . ." It sounded like Radd said "the cavalry," but Bill blanked out. When he was aware again, there seemed to be a bunch of people in the men's room, including at least two women. Bill guessed they were Maybell and Marguerite. His eyes were closed, and he heard it all as if in a dream. Someone wanted to move him out of the bathroom. Someone else wanted to check for broken bones first. Bill had heard about broken bones before and felt excited at the prospect of experiencing one.

Then he was aware of being carried. He was set down somewhere. The sound of the bowling was louder. They were making him sit up. That hurt, and he wished they wouldn't do that. The stabbing pain woke him up and made him long for the numbness again. He gratefully sank into it, but they kept talking to him, even shouting, insisting he leave it behind.

He felt cold on his face and heard Maybell say, "I need more ice."

Someone said, "He's bleeding," to which Maybell responded, "The ice'll help with that."

Maybell spoke right into Bill's ear, "Who did this, Bill?"

Bill felt his head turning, could almost make her out as if from a distance. But all this seemed more like a dream than life, and he didn't try to answer.

Someone came with more ice. Despite the cold, Bill drifted back into the numbness. Then he was being helped by several people into Maybell's truck. And then Maybell was helping him onto his cot in Sonny Boy's room.

"Maybe you wanna pee first."

But Bill gratefully gave in to the numbness again.

Now at three-thirty the numbness was completely gone. He felt pain in almost every part of his body. Too much pain for him to get up. Too much for him to sleep.

Thoughts started coming quickly. The furious girl. The sudden smell of the bottom of her boot. The stars that lit up the inside of his head. How in one moment life turns from something good to something awful.

This was the human experience he dreaded. The reason he stayed back as long as he did. The seemingly infinite ways that hate could be expressed and that pain could be felt. Of course people were friendly to him. People were always friendly until they turned on you. He had watched it happen again and again, but from a distance. Even though he knew it, he still forgot it could happen to him. He got caught up, just like everyone else. He wondered, with a growing sense of panic, what else he had forgotten.

He longed to escape into sleep. But he was wide awake now.

"I am this body," he thought. There was no avoiding it anymore. The body was screaming at him. There was nothing as loud in the whole world. It screamed and it wouldn't stop screaming.

Seconds dripped by slowly, taking an eternity to form a minute. One minute in an endless sea of minutes.

"I am this body. This body is me."

Bill didn't know what time he had fallen asleep again. When he opened his eyes there was the faintest hint of gray in the room. He knew he hadn't slept long. It was the first time since being there that he had no awareness while he was sleeping. There was no floating. No glowing string. He had simply been unconscious.

He thought of the stories he heard, how others had come like him into a human body. And how they got lost in the experience, forgetting themselves, living out the rest of their body's lifespan. Perhaps they became so accustomed to thinking of themselves as human that, even after dying, they fell into the cycle of rebirth and death like the rest of us.

Before, Bill had imagined that their forgetting happened slowly; a gradual identification with their human shell. But now he understood that it was sudden. It might have been pleasure that did it, like with love. But more likely it was pain. Pain was so loud, so consuming, so terrifying. Either of them, pleasure or pain, were way too powerful for anyone to contend with. Newborns didn't stand a chance. And Bill finally realized that he didn't either. Pain had defeated him.

"I am this body," he thought.

As he lay there, he realized what was coming next. There was another force in this world that would soon be acting on him. And like the forces of pleasure and pain, it would be irresistible. There could be no planetary life without it.

It was the instinct to survive. He couldn't say when it would overtake him, but he knew for sure that it would. Probably soon.

When it did, the way out would be closed to him. Bill would be unable to end his life.

Maybell stirred in her sleep. I guess she had some pretty good radar, because even though there was no sound, she knew someone was in her room. It was still mostly dark, nearly five a.m., shortly before she normally woke up. She turned to her door and saw Bill.

"Bill, we got fifteen minutes. Lemme sleep."

She sunk her head back down and drifted.

"I didn't want it to get like this," he said. "That was the whole point."

"It's early . . ."

"I never understood why you do this. You don't have to. No one has to. Why do you put yourselves through this?"

"Bill . . ." Maybell folded her pillow over her head. "Shush."

"I just came to say good-bye. I have to return something and then I'm leaving."

Bill turned and left the room. Maybell lifted her head, suddenly awake now.

"Wait? What? Bill?"

She got out of bed, putting on her robe. She went out to the living room.

"Bill?"

She found him leaving Sonny Boy's room. He was wearing the clothes he'd had on when he arrived.

"Bill, you can't just go. I need you. You're my cook."

Bill walked to the front door. Maybell followed.

"Look Bill, I know you got dinged up. I'm sorry. But you can't just walk away."

Bill got to the door and opened it. Maybell put herself in his way.

"Listen to me. Just listen to me. Okay?"

He paused in the doorway.

"Look," she said, "It's too late for me to hire another cook. You walk out, I got no diner. Don't leave me high and dry. Just one day. Gimme one day to figure this out."

Maybell wanted more than a day. She wanted every day. But he was at the edge, and she knew this was all she could ask. She'd figure out the rest later.

"One day won't kill ya—right? You can leave tomorrow morning. Hell, I'll drive you wherever you wanna go. Just gimme the day, Bill."

Bill hesitated. He didn't want to do anything to hurt Maybell. "Okay," he said.

"Thank you Bill. Thank you. Stay right here. I'll get changed. Won't take me a minute."

Bill was too close to the door for Maybell's comfort. She hurried into her room.

For a few moments he stood like a ghost, neither here nor there. That's how it was he didn't notice me. But I heard the whole thing. When Maybell left, I went up behind him.

"I know why you're going," I said.

He didn't turn to face me. He kept his gaze outside the door. That's where he wanted to be.

"It's this town," I went on. "It sucks the life out of you."

I had decided as much last night when Maybell brought Bill back.

I had heard her pull up and then struggle to get Bill out of the truck. I went out and helped her get him inside and then onto the cot. After she went off to bed, I sat by Bill's side for a while. As I watched him sleep, I began to wonder if I could do that cooking trick on him. Look into him and see what it was he wanted. It's not that I was out to cook him anything. I just wanted to see more of him than I had.

So I closed my eyes and began to breathe slowly in and out. I pictured Bill's face in my mind. But I got nothing. I figured Bill was like some of those people in the diner I couldn't read at all. I opened my eyes and looked at that swollen red face. Slowly, an idea dawned on me. I don't know what made me think of it. But I closed my eyes again and pictured him. Instead of trying to guess what Bill wanted, I tried to guess what he didn't want.

That's when the floodgates opened. I saw hatred. And anger. Meanness. Brutality. I saw something about Bill I never would have guessed. He was actually the most scared person I had ever known. I do believe that Bill dreaded this world more than I did. And when I saw that, when I saw how frightened he was, and how tender, I was flooded with love for him.

Both of us wanted to be someplace else. Someplace without broken people. Without the cruelty that stands in place of love. Someplace that wasn't Hadley.

As Bill stood now at the front door, looking out, everything in his being was screaming to go. Everything in me was screaming the same thing.

I tried to sound casual, but it was hard. "I know you wanna leave," I said, "As it happens, I feel the same way. Maybe we can go together." I took Bill's hand in mine. He closed his eyes a moment, and I saw a tear come down his cheek. With the benefit of hindsight I might have interpreted that tear in any number of ways. For instance, maybe Bill had been moved by a tender gesture. Or Bill was still in pain from the beating last night. Maybe he had just seen a chick flick. The point is, it turns out I'm as much inclined as anyone to see what I want to see. And that morning I chose to see that Bill was in love with me too.

I was totally clear about what we had to do. I leaned in and spoke softly, so there was no way Maybell could hear, "I'll make all the arrangements. You don't have to worry about a thing. I'll get us tickets. Everything. I'm gonna find us a place, Bill. A place we can be." I got on my tiptoes to whisper right in his ear. "I love you."

It took a long while for those words to get through the haze of Bill's pain. By the time he turned around, I was already in my bedroom, packing.

Maybell rushed out of her room and took Bill by the arm.

"Let's go, Bill."

She led him out the door.

The line to get into Maybell's was even longer than yesterday. Maybell was too busy to see me enter, so there was no way she would have noticed I didn't have my schoolbooks. I wouldn't need them anymore. It didn't surprise me that I wasn't staying to graduate. The point was never to get a diploma. That piece of paper was only a permission slip to leave town for good. And I wasn't waiting for permission any longer.

Between the last booth and the restrooms, I buckled Clover into his bubble walker and looked him in the eyes. I was surprised when my own eyes welled up. This was going to be the hardest part.

"You're gonna be okay," I told him. "You pulled a low card with Maybell. Sonny Boy's basically awright. He'll take care of you. You may wind up with another brother or sister. Try not to let Maybell mess 'em up." I gave Clover a tight hug. For all the pain I had felt in that house, that baby had become attached to my heart like an extra chamber and I was never going to see him again.

As I left, I saw Bill at the grill, his back to the customers. He was slumping and I could tell he was miserable. This town had that effect on everyone. But I felt better knowing he'd be getting out.

Despite myself I took one last look at Maybell. She was refilling coffees at a table and leaving a check. As last looks go, it wasn't too bad. Better than seeing her head out for the night to get wasted and laid.

When I left the diner and passed by Harley's truck, it didn't register to me at the time that he wasn't sitting on his tailgate, as he had taken to doing lately. Instead, he was inside the cab. And his truck wasn't parked facing away from Maybell's. It was facing forward. Even if I had noticed, I wouldn't have known why that mattered.

Harley was already mostly through his first six pack of the day. The cab was littered as always with empty beer cans and junk food wrappers, loose receipts and such. But there was something new. It was a small bag from Brighton Sporting Goods. It hadn't yet been opened. And there was something else: Harley's rifle, which always sat on the rack behind him, was recently cleaned and loaded.

Martin entered from the kitchen carrying a tray with clean glasses. He loaded them on a shelf by the soda dispenser. Rose took two right off the shelf and dunked them in the ice bin to fill them up. While she poured iced-tea into the first, she spoke to Martin without looking at him.

"What've you got, Martin?"

Martin looked confused. "Glasses . . ."

"What disease have you got? I know you're sick." Rose filled the next glass with Diet Coke.

"It's a few things at this point. But the most pressing is cancer." This was no place to talk about it, and yet Martin was glad to tell someone. "It's spread to my bones."

Rose tried not to show emotion. She took two straws out of her pocket to create more time to talk. Normally, they'd come out at the table. "How long have you got?"

"Not long."

Rose didn't talk for a long moment. She couldn't move.

"Rose," Martin said by way of explaining. "I didn't come here to start a romance."

She turned to him in anger. "Then why did you come here?!"

Martin thought of the kiss last night. He had been so focused on dying that he hadn't given the tiniest space in his mind for living. Rose had taken him by surprise. As he looked at her searching eyes, he thought she deserved to know.

"I came because of Bill. That article about him? I think Bill knows something." He was reluctant, but he had to tell her now. "I think he knows what happens when we die."

Again, her body wouldn't move. She tried and then realized she couldn't control it. Martin stepped toward her and reached for her arm. That snapped her out of it.

"Don't!" she yelled, pulling back. "I can't do this! I already lost one husband. I can't live through that again!"

Rose was furious that her eyes were filling with tears. Martin looked like a fuzzy mass. Then again, it was a relief not to see his face. She turned and walked away, forgetting the drink order.

She passed by a young man at the front of the line who tried to get her attention. He was hoping to get a seat at the counter, close to the cook. His right hand sat in his jacket pocket, gripping a paring knife.

I sat across from the bank officer at Hadley Trust. His name was Nick Wallace. He was in his mid-forties, I figured, with thinning gray hair and a belly that his jacket couldn't hide. He passed me the form to sign. I didn't have to close my account in order to get all the money out. But I thought it would be poetic if I did.

"Sorry to lose your business," he said in a generic friendly way. I'm sure one look at me told him there was never going to be much business. Some people have spent so much of their lives acting pleasant, they don't how to shut it off. Their routine is like a screw that's been loosened so many times, it's lost its threads.

He counted out my money surprisingly fast, considering his fat fingers. I figured he must have started out as a teller.

"So, eight hundred, nine hundred, twenty, forty, sixty-five, and thirty-one cents."

That was my life savings, scraped together from babysitting, odd jobs, squirreling away my allowance for the day I'd be leaving this town.

"That's a lot of money," he said.

"You kidding?" I stood up and put it in my pocket. I doubted it would last us a week.

"Well, it was in my day," he smiled.

Why do people insist on being relentlessly positive? I gave Nick Wallace my best grim look and left without a word. If people want to see the world as sunny, far be it for me to rain on them.

Next, I went to the Hadley Library a block down. Most of its books were donated, but they had a fairly new computer with internet access. I logged on and got the bus schedule between Hadley and Phoenix. And then the flight schedule between Phoenix and anywhere else. I figured the farther Bill and I got, the less likely anyone would bother us. Seattle looked good. I had heard there were islands off the coast. I wondered if we could find one that was uninhabited.

I had Maybell's credit card info memorized. But when I tried to book us plane tickets, I saw that I needed Bill's birthdate.

I was iffy on Bill not having been born. If he said he wasn't, okay. I wouldn't argue. My thinking was he just didn't fit into this upside-down world, and there was no better reason for us to be together. But Southwest Airlines insisted on having his birthdate. I guessed that Bill had on him, somewhere, some kind of ID. Which meant that the birthdate I entered had to be accurate.

So I put the computer to sleep. Like it or not, I had to go back to the diner.

People at the diner were forgiving at first. It sort of went like this: "I thought I wanted over-easy, but if Bill made me scrambled, maybe that's what my soul needed." Bill had earned a lot of slack, especially from the locals. And let's face it, diner food is pretty much all the same anyway.

But then orders started going really wrong. Like Mrs. Newman getting a side of bacon when everyone knows she's vegetarian. And a diabetic mom from out of town getting a hot chocolate. A buzz was starting to go around the diner, like you might hear on a cruise ship when people started noticing an iceberg.

Bill was seized by fear. What was once easy now seemed impossible, as if there was a door he had access to that had suddenly disappeared and he could no longer find it. The harder he tried, the deeper his panic grew. Before, when people got their orders mind-read, they would look at Bill with awe. With love, really. He feared what might replace that love that if he no longer gave them what they wanted. And underneath that fear, a new thought was stirring. It took time to take shape, as he actively didn't want to face it. But soon Bill stared head-on at the possibility—at the likelihood, really—that he had already forgotten everything he knew before becoming Bill. Forgotten even what he had forgotten.

Maybell stepped up to get his attention. "Bill?"

He didn't look up. She put a hand gently on his shoulder.

Bill stopped working and looked at her. His face seemed more swollen now, probably from the heat of the grill.

"What's the matter?" she asked.

He just shook his head and turned back to the grill.

"Bill, look, you're just having a bad day, that's all. After last night, who can blame you? Tell you what, you just worry about cooking. We'll bring you the orders."

Bill nodded. But he didn't feel relief. He felt defeat.

Maybell motioned for Dolene and Rose to come join her. They met up near the utility drawer. Maybell reached in and got three pads.

"We're gonna be taking orders this morning. Rose, you've never done that before, but it's easy."

Rose nodded.

"What if people don't want that?" Dolene asked.

"Then they can go get egg burritos at the Chevron."

Maybell took a pen from her pocket and went to table 7. "Hi folks, what can I get ya?"

Cyril had been seated at the counter, but too far from the grill. He was all the way by the kitchen door. Nothing was going right on this trip.

The night before, Katie had been especially cold to him. She wasn't in the room when he got back from the party and later when she did get back, she was like a different person. He could tell she had been crying. And sex was definitely out. Katie wasn't saying anything, but Cyril knew in his gut that it was over. Whatever part of her that he'd been able to connect with was gone. Thank you, fucking Peter.

Katie was snoring beside him when he woke up that morning. He slipped out quietly.

Now he was looking at some old lady who was taking his order. Fine. He asked for the cheapest thing on the menu, scrambled eggs, no potatoes. That bullshit about mind-reading orders, that was probably so they could make everyone get the most expensive thing. Just a scam.

Cyril thought he'd skip out right then, get in his car and go back to Phoenix. Leave Katie there. It would serve her right. Who the hell wanted to eat eggs that Peter cooked anyway?

And then it happened. Peter walked right by him on his way into the kitchen. Didn't even look over. Cyril's hand felt for the handle of the knife. Peter was going to have to come back through that door.

Maybell hadn't made any calls to find a new cook, as she had promised Bill she would. And she sure wasn't going to give Harley his job back. Who could possibly replace a mind-reading grill cook?

Maybell had gotten used to the crowds in the diner. She liked the look of surprise on the teller's face when she made her deposits. Money meant options, and Maybell enjoyed having them. She liked feeling that her diner was the center of the world.

Bill was a man and she knew men. She knew men better than they knew themselves. She couldn't get Oren to stay, but Oren was different. He was a wild horse like her. If there was ever a man built for the corral, it was Bill.

And then she saw him walk into the kitchen to get some more supplies. This was as good a chance as any.

Once again I walked right by Harley's truck without noticing. If I had bothered to look in, I probably still wouldn't have realized what he was up to.

Harley tore open the Brighton's bag and took out his new ski mask. There wasn't any skiing around Hadley, but people would drive out to the mountains to see snow. Harley put the hat on and pulled the mask part down. He was blinded at first, drunkenly tugging at the mask, trying to get the eyeholes to line up.

Bill had gone to the kitchen for some more cheese and butter, but when Maybell found him he was at the far end of the prep table, back to the diner, staring into space.

"You okay, Bill?"

Bill didn't turn or answer.

"Bill, I've been thinking about everything you said. And I'm just wondering, do you really have to go? If you think about it, there's nothing keeping you from staying here."

Bill stayed silent.

Maybell added some flirt into her voice. "I don't mean just in town. I mean . . . with me. We're together all the time. Work under the same roof. Live under the same roof. You ever think about me, Bill? Sometimes, I think about you."

Now Maybell moved closer, her hand brushing along the stainless steel table like it was a large, rectangular penis and she was showing off her mastery over that organ, no matter its shape or size.

She leaned close and whispered in his ear so he could feel her breath, "Do you think you could ever be attracted to me?"

His lips were still swollen, and she didn't want her kiss to be associated with any kind of pain. So she kissed him so gently, as to barely be felt. That somehow made it more sexual.

I saw it from the kitchen door.

The sight of Maybell seducing Bill could not have been a more perfect ending to my miserable childhood. It's like Maybell had been working from the Encyclopedia of Ways To Ruin Your Daughter, page by page over the years, and now she just skipped to the last chapter. She was a perfect, destroying machine.

"I can't believe you!" I yelled from behind them. "Is there some way you haven't ruined my life?!"

Maybell was saying something, but she was already dead to me, and her words came out like empty air. I went up to Bill. "How could you?! I love you!"

I slapped Bill hard on the side of his face that Katie had kicked in the night before. I wanted him to feel it, and he did. Tears were coming down his cheeks.

I heard Maybell gasp and saw a look of horror on her face. At first I thought it was because of the slap or because I fell for an older man. But I realized it was something else. All her life, Maybell had been able to get any guy she wanted, no matter what woman had a claim. That was her superpower. It bothered her conscience no more than it bothered a spider to trap a fly. But taking a guy from her own daughter, the first guy her daughter ever wanted, that broke some unwritten code. It bit right through her.

"Baby, I didn't know. I swear I didn't."

"Shut up!" I yelled it at the top of my lungs. It was almost a scream. "Shut up!"

Now things were happening fast. Out in his truck, Harley got tired of fishing around for the eyeholes in the ski mask.

"Fuck it," he muttered.

He pulled off the whole thing. He started his engine and grabbed the rifle off the rack behind him.

Maybell followed me out into the diner. She put her hand on my shoulder as I was halfway to the door. I swung around and knocked her hand away.

"Don't touch me! You're a bitch an' a whore and all you care about is you!"

"Baby, I swear, if I had known . . ."

I could see Rose out of the corner of my eye. She was like a deer in headlights. So was Martin. With everyone distracted by me, no one noticed Cyril pulling the knife out of his pocket.

Bill stepped back in from the kitchen. If anyone but Cyril had bothered to look at him, they would have seen a resigned look on his face. He felt an ending was coming at him fast. He welcomed it. He closed his eyes.

Cyril would never have a more perfect moment. Everyone was looking at the owner and her daughter. And Peter was helpless. Cyril stood up and made a fist around the knife so he could drive it hard into Peter's chest. That's when the first shots were fired.

Glass was shattering. The front panes blew into pieces. People instinctively dove under tables or just hit the floor.

Maybell dragged me down, which when you think about it, pretty much sums up my life with her. After the first few rounds were fired, I looked up to see the source. It was a girl, not much older than me, the one I had seen in the car.

Katie stood outside the diner. With the glass blown out, she had a direct line of fire at Bill.

Cyril was on the floor. He saw Katie outside holding the gun he had brought to Hadley. He crept back away from Bill. He knew if Katie saw him, he'd be a target too.

Harley heard the shots just as he was ready to gun it for the diner. He pulled his rifle back inside and didn't bother to rack it, even though it was loaded. He turned and sped off.

Bill stood alone. I think he knew this made him a clear target. That's what he wanted. He even came from behind the counter, so Katie wouldn't miss. It was probably no more than four seconds that had passed, but it felt like a lifetime to me. Bill gave Katie a nod. She raised the gun.

As she looked at Bill, a new thought went across her face. Bill knew instantly what it was. He shook his head. Before he could shout for her to stop, Katie turned the gun to her own temple and pulled the trigger.

The people outside who had been on line, crouching to keep out of the way, collectively gasped.

But instead of an explosion of sound and blood, there was just a *Click*.

Katie looked at the empty gun in her hand.

"That so figures."

In that instant she was tackled from behind, her spine arching backwards, the gun flying from her hand. It was Chief Munt. His right knee pinned Katie's right arm behind her back. His left boot squeezed her left hand painfully into the ground. With his left hand he pushed her face into the gravel. With the other he got out his handcuffs.

The Chief didn't notice the young man running away from the diner, or see the paring knife drop from his hand.

I had imagined that Maybell's Diner after the shooting was like a ship that had run aground. People started to get themselves off the floor and looked around to see what had happened. Some had small cuts from the glass or the impact of hitting thecj188

floor. Plates were knocked over and many people had bits of food on them. I don't think I heard a word spoken. Loved ones checked each other. Some of them embraced.

Rose was on the floor behind the counter. In the chaos of the shooting, her foot had caught on the rubber floor mat. She fell and hit her head on the lower shelf under the counter. She'd get a bump, but the skin didn't break. Unlike the others, she didn't know the shooter had been stopped. It wasn't until Martin helped her up that she knew it was over. When she looked beyond the counter, she saw people starting to wipe themselves off. Some were leaving. Then she reflected on the gentleness with which Martin had come to her aid. She turned to thank him, but he was already out of sight.

Before I could get bearings of any kind, I felt Maybell next to me getting herself up. It was her diner, and I guess she felt responsible, like the captain of a ship. Once she was sure the shooter had been cuffed, she went around and helped customers to their feet. She was worried someone had been hit. Luckily no one was.

When I lifted my head up, a couple passed by in front of me, and I could see across the diner. Bill had taken a seat at the counter. I think he was the only one sitting. His back was to the window and he looked as if he was waiting for someone to pour him some coffee.

I don't remember going outside. I must have followed the crowd. I remember seeing the Chief putting Katie into his squad car, just like on TV, hand over her head. I got a good look at her face, still puffy from crying. Another girl betrayed by Bill.

I wasn't walking to any place in particular. I didn't have any place to go. Not anymore. I was rudderless.

Then I heard Maybell. She had stepped outside the diner and was calling for me, searching. And just like that, I had a purpose. To get away. I had just started walking when she spotted me.

"Belutha! Belutha! You okay?"

I didn't turn. I didn't stop. I just walked. No way I was ever going to let her touch me again.

The Chief sat in the back seat next to Katie and talked with her for some time. Outside the car, the Deputy did what he was told, which was to just wait. He wondered what was going on in the car. And would he get his head taken off if he knocked on the window to ask for a pee break. Then the door opened. The Chief got out.

"Kip, keep an eye on the suspect. I'll be back." Without explanation, the Chief walked into the diner.

The place had mostly cleared out. It wasn't hard to find Bill. He was still seated at the counter. The Chief wiped the glass off a stool next to him and sat down.

"Bill."

He didn't get a response.

"I suppose you know that girl was shooting at you."

Again, Bill didn't say anything.

"According to her, she knows you. Katie Dyson. Does that name ring a bell?"

Bill just shook his head.

"Say Bill, I wonder if you'd mind coming to the station with me."

Bill looked at the Chief for the first time. He nodded.

"Let's go," the Chief said, rising.

Bill followed him outside.

They got to the Chief's car, where the Deputy stood guard.

"Kip," the Chief said. "Bill's gonna ride to the station in your car. He's a voluntary witness."

"Sure thing, Chief."

The Deputy's car was now parked nearby. As he led Bill over, Maybell ran up. "Hey, Bill, where're you going?"

The Deputy looked at the Chief for direction. The Chief motioned for him to keep going, then stood between Maybell and the Deputy's squad car.

"Maybell," he said, "I just wanna have a talk with Bill."

"What the hell for?"

"You can come down to the station a little later."

Bill got into the squad car. The Deputy closed the door and got in himself. The Chief took off with Katie, and the Deputy followed.

Rodney had spent nearly an hour negotiating with Phil of Phil's Auto Body to get the price down on a blown-out Suzuki FS 1. It had been sitting out in the back for the last couple of years. Rodney figured he could fix it up and get maybe nine hundred bucks for it, or at least get his money back in parts. While they haggled, two police cars and an ambulance sped by, but the guys barely noticed. Finally, they settled on a hundred eighty bucks.

Phil helped Rodney heft it into the back of his truck, then got back to work. Rodney started to tie it down. He went to loop the rope through the handle of the passenger door and that's when he saw me sitting inside his truck. He jumped back.

"Belutha?"

I had no idea where I was going when I walked away from May-bell's. The only thing on my mind was to just keep walking. After a mile I noticed Rodney's truck outside Phil's. Instantly, I knew what to do.

The window was down. I looked at Rodney.

"I'm ready, Rodney."

He just stared.

"Get in," I said. "Let's go."

"Go where?"

"I said I'm ready."

Rodney wasn't sure what that meant, but I could almost read his mind as the possibility of having sex fired the neurons in the lizard portion of his brain. He gave a *whoop* and threw the rest of the rope back into the bed, no longer caring about the Suzuki.

He got in and drove us off.

"Brains are slow. They're made of matter, which means thought has to pass from one physical point to another.

"Actual thought doesn't use matter. That's why it happens instantaneously.

"Actual thought perceives actual reality. Brains perceive planet reality.

"Your belief that your brains can perceive actual reality is really the most poetic example of how limited they are."

—*Bill Bill, Interview at Maybell's Diner*

Bill sat alone in the holding room of the Hadley Police Station. There wasn't anything there but a table and two chairs. I guess that was the idea. If they had magazines or a TV, suspects wouldn't be panicking and getting ready to confess everything they'd done.

But Bill did have something to look at. It was a mirror, the see-through kind like on TV. In the twenty minutes that Bill sat alone in that room, he couldn't stop staring at his own reflection.

The door opened from the outside and Chief Munt entered, holding a file folder.

"Hey, Bill," he said friendly enough. "Thanks for waiting."

Bill kept looking at his own reflection.

"I had a talk with that girl who shot at ya. Katie. Hell hath no fury. You know what I mean?"

Bill had no response.

"She says you two had quite the romance. She says you almost died of an opioid overdose. Actually, she said you did die, briefly. I called Phoenix Memorial and they confirmed that. Does any of this sound familiar?"

Bill shook his head.

"Well, I need you to stay here for now."

Munt slid his chair out and stood. Bill looked at him for the first time.

"I want to go."

"You just sit tight. I'll be back."

The Chief left the room and closed the door. He double-checked to make sure it was locked.

Maybell, Rose, and Martin were in the lobby, giving the young Deputy at the front desk a pretty good reason to regret joining the force.

"What do you mean we can't see him?" Maybell yelled. "He didn't do the shooting! He was the one they were goddam shootin' at! Is that what you do in this town? Arrest the victim? Someone breaks into my diner, you gonna arrest me?"

The Deputy looked up at Maybell. There was something creepy about being yelled at by a woman in a waitress uniform. It made him feel like a boy.

"Ma'am . . . ," he started.

"Do not even *think* about 'ma'aming' me! I know my rights."

"Actually, ma'am—actually, those rights apply to people in custody."

Rose leaned forward to the young Deputy. "Are you even old enough to be a policeman?"

The door to the inner station opened. Chief Munt came out and the Deputy let out a sigh.

"Folks," the Chief said to Maybell and the others. "Come with me, please. I'll tell ya everything that's going on."

He held the door open. Maybell and Martin went inside. Rose followed, after a huff at the Deputy.

The Chief led them all to his small office, bringing an extra chair from the next room. The Chief went behind his desk and sat. He had that same file folder. Now he opened it.

"Maybell . . ." The Chief took a pause. This was going to take some tact. "You need to prepare yourself for a shock. The man you know as Bill Bill is not who you think. Bill is his alias. His real name is Peter Swaine."

The room was silent. Maybell looked at Rose. Their expressions showed there was no way they believed that. The Chief expected that reaction. He took some photos from the file folder and laid them on his desk so they faced the others. The pictures showed Bill in various younger ages. They were all mug shots.

"He's wanted in Phoenix for possession and distribution of methamphetamine and oxycodone."

Maybell looked at the photos. They were clearly Bill. She couldn't speak.

Rose held one in her hand, then plunked it down, as if it was obviously fake. "Is this where our tax money goes?"

The Chief was aware that he and Maybell went back. When he went through his divorce eight years before, Maybell gave him free coffee and an ear. It had helped. He knew this was going to be hard. He tried to soften his tone.

"There's more. At 3:43 a.m. on the fourteenth of last month, Peter was admitted to Phoenix Memorial Hospital with an opioid overdose. He was pronounced dead at . . ." Here the Chief had to check his file. "At 4:32 a.m. Now here's the thing. Fifty-two minutes after that, at 5:24, Peter got up and walked out of the hospital. It's on the surveillance tape."

Another silence. Among the photos in front of them, Maybell saw the surveillance shots of Bill leaving the hospital. They had a time/date stamp. She passed them to Rose and Martin. The Chief broke the silence.

"I'll tell you what I think. People have been known to come back after being legally dead. It's been documented. But sometimes, if the brain goes long enough without oxygen, there can be damage." He let that sink in a moment. "I believe that's what happened to Peter. It's my opinion that Peter Swaine *believes* he's Bill Bill."

Rose looked thoughtful. "You're saying Bill's crazy?"

That hung in the air.

"That's for an expert to decide," the Chief finally said.

Maybell looked Munt in the eyes. Ever since he became Chief, he had always acted like a gentleman. During three of those years, when he was unmarried, he never once tried to hit on her. If he believed something, she knew you had better take it seriously.

Now it was Martin who broke the silence. "There may be another explanation," he said. "You remember that article that was written about Bill? Have you considered that maybe it was true?"

"No, I have not," the Chief replied.

"May I ask why?"

"Because aliens don't show up and take over the bodies of dead people. At least not in Hadley, so far as I know."

Martin was going to argue that Bill never said he was an alien. And that this wasn't the stuff of science fiction. But he'd taught enough students to know when his audience was not going to be receptive. He sat back in his chair.

The Chief went on. "Now here's what's gonna happen. I've alerted the Phoenix authorities that Peter Swaine's in custody. Tomorrow morning first thing, I'm going to drive him to the South Mountain Police Precinct where Peter will be processed and held for trail."

There was a long silence. No one knew what to say.

The Chief went on: "I've got him sitting in a holding room right now. You folks can see him one more time, if you want."

When Maybell saw Bill sitting at that table, she flashed back to the first day she met him at the diner. She hadn't thought twice about bringing him home, having him stay in the house with her kids, sharing a room with her thirteen-year-old. Yeah, she knew she'd never win Mother of the Year. But now when she looked at him, dressed in the greasy clothes he arrived in, bruised from a beating, it seemed like he belonged in a police holding room. How could she have not seen that before?

Bill didn't look up as Munt led Maybell and the others into the room. His eyes were fixed on the mirror.

"Peter . . .?"

Bill sat silently, so the Chief began again.

"Bill . . . Your friends have come to say good-bye."

Bill didn't turn, but he looked down and blinked. Rose figured he must have felt ashamed.

"Hey, Bill," Maybell began. But then she was at a loss for what more to say. She and Rose exchanged a look.

Martin turned to Munt and gestured to a chair. "Do you mind?"

The Chief shook his head. Martin sat across from Bill. He didn't realize how weak his legs felt until then.

"Bill?" Martin paused for Bill to look at him. Bill didn't, so Martin went on anyway. "I'm about out of time. I think you are too. It's got to be now. Bill, you promised you would help me. You said when the time came . . . you said you'd be there."

Bill didn't turn away from his reflection, but by the way he blinked, Martin knew Bill could hear him. Martin leaned in. He didn't want the others to hear this, but he had no choice.

"Bill, what's going to happen? Am I going to be nothing? Is that all this comes to? Does any of this have a point?" And when Bill said nothing, Martin's voice grew desperate. "Bill . . ."

Rose felt a tear go down her face. Was this how Jessie felt? It had been so long since he died that, when she thought about him, it was only in terms of herself: her loss, her loneliness. She had forgotten completely what Jessie had gone through. Now here it was in front of her again: a man facing his end.

Bill finally looked over at Martin. "I'm lost, Martin. Like you. I can't help you anymore." Bill looked back at his face in the mirror. "I am this body. This body is me," he said to himself.

"I don't understand," Martin said, shaking his head.

Bill finally admitted, "I stayed too long."

Maybell remembered that morning. Bill wanted to leave, and she had talked him out of it. It seemed so long ago. He wouldn't be sitting there, soon to be extradited to Phoenix, if she hadn't stopped him.

"Bill, please," Martin tried one more time.

Bill just stared at the mirror.

The Chief took a step forward. "Okay, folks, it's time to go."

Maybell put a hand on Martin's shoulder. He stood reluctantly. Bill looked at the Chief.

"Not you, Peter. You're going to Phoenix tomorrow."

"I'm not Peter," Bill said with a hopelessness that Maybell could feel in her gut.

The Chief led the others out.

I sat in the cab while Rodney went inside. I'd passed this house plenty of times, but never knew it was his. His mom was a craft artist who made lawn knickknacks she tried to sell at fairs. I don't think she ever made much money. Their yard was a graveyard of her unsold work. Rodney's dad worked odd jobs, mostly carpentry, but sometimes on engines.

It wasn't long before Rodney came out of the house with a khaki canvas bag loaded with his stuff.

A few hours earlier I was set to begin my life with a man I loved. And instead I was going off with a guy who dreamed of nothing but car engines and sex with me.

Maybell had taken years to compromise her soul. I sold mine outright in one afternoon.

Deputy Kiplowski was told he could wait in the squad car. But there was no explicit order against him standing outside Maybell's. The diner had been roped off with yellow police tape. No one was allowed in or out. When the first camera truck came, the Deputy realized that if he stood guard outside, he would wind up in the shot. The news crew didn't seem to mind him standing there, in fact they positioned their camera to get him in the foreground. Between TV trucks, the Deputy called his mom and sister and friends to let them know which channel to watch.

By late afternoon most of the visitors in town had left. Some took pictures of the diner before driving off, or selfies with the diner in the background. The Deputy saw no harm and didn't try to stop them. Most of the pilgrims had left too. Some had knocked on Kip's window to ask when the diner would reopen. Kip said the same thing to everyone: the diner was closed indefinitely. That was the Chief's wording. Munt hoped it would sound discouraging enough to cause people to leave town. And it did.

As each visitor drove away, the Deputy grew a little nostalgic. It had been exciting in Hadley for a while.

A woman marching toward him broke his reverie. She made no signs of slowing. When he realized it was Maybell, Kip's hand went instinctively to his holster. He was embarrassed and hoped she didn't notice.

"Ma'am, no one's allowed inside the diner. Police orders." He planned to say "Chief's orders," but thought the word "police" would sound more official.

Maybell didn't even slow down. "It's my diner, and I'm gettin' my stuff. You wanna shoot me, feel free." She went under the police line.

"Ma'am! Ma'am, you can't . . ." And then she was inside the diner. The Deputy looked around and tried to seem casual, as if he had intended to let Maybell inside. He was grateful the TV trucks were gone.

It was like a bomb had gone off in there. A few hours ago her diner had felt like the center of the world. Now it seemed dead. There was broken glass, overturned chairs, dishes on the floor, food everywhere. And there was the silence. That was the most striking.

The Chief had given no indication when she could reopen. She couldn't even think about who she would hire after Bill. It was as if nearly twenty years of owning a diner, a whole portion of her life, was suddenly over.

She opened the cash register. Nothing had been taken. That was impressive. Maybell found a plastic bag and emptied the cash into it. She didn't bother with the change. She found another bag and put the whole tip jar inside. She shut off the gas to the grill in case some vagrant decided to sneak in and cook a meal.

In the utility drawer she pulled out a few key papers and added them to the bag. Then she remembered the gun. She took that out and put it in the bag.

If the Deputy wanted to look inside, he could just screw himself.

Rodney stayed in the truck while I went inside Maybell's house. I had started to pack earlier, so I didn't need long.

Maybell had arranged for Sonny Boy to leave school early to babysit Clover. He came into my room while I emptied the drawers. Normally he would never do that without my permission. He knew something was up.

"Where're you goin'?" he said simply.

"I'm leavin'. For good. Maybe go start my own family."

"I thought you were a lesbian."

"That was last week."

I kept packing, and he kept standing there. I thought about what would happen after I left and how it would all fall on him; the baby, managing Maybell. I stopped a moment and turned to him.

"Look, Sonny Boy, I'm sorry I never really got to know you. It wasn't 'cause you were from another father. I don't care about that. I can't even stand my own. I just . . . have issues, you know?"

He nodded. "Yeah, I know."

I knelt on top of my bag and squeezed the zipper shut around me.

Sonny Boy sat down on my bed, which would have been another infraction in normal times. He took off his left shoe and reached under the insole. He had a bunch of bills laid flat, about ninety bucks. He offered it all to me.

"You might need that."

There was a simple innocence on his face. It took me leaving for good to finally see my half-brother was a decent guy. How ridiculous this was, all of it. I shook my head.

"You keep it. You'll need it more." I got my bag off the bed. "Don't let Maybell push you around," I said. Then, stopping at my door, I turned back. "And *don't* let her reproduce!"

When I got outside, Maybell was pulling up. I threw my bag in the back of Rodney's truck and stood to face my mother as she marched up to me.

"Belutha? What's going on?"

"I'm leaving. Me and Rodney. We're going away."

Rodney had gotten out to meet Maybell. He held his hand outstretched. "Hey, Miss Mariah. I'm Rodney Haas. Glad to meet you . . ."

Maybell ignored him and got right in my face. "You're not going anywhere."

That almost made me laugh. "Who's gonna stop me? You?" I started for the Rodney's passenger door. "Let's go, Rodney."

"What about Bill?" she said. "You know he's goin' to jail. They're taking him to Phoenix in the morning."

That was news. A hundred questions flooded my mind, but I wasn't going to ask Maybell.

"Nothing I can do about that," I said. I got in the cab. "Let's go, Rodney."

Rodney gave Maybell a polite smile and came around to get in.

Maybell was flustered. "What are you gonna do? Where're you gonna go?"

"Who cares?!" I yelled. "Maybe I'll start squeezing out babies like you did. Worked for you—right?"

Rodney piped in, "I think we should talk about this."

"Go, Rodney!"

He hesitated.

I yelled, "Go!"

He put the truck in gear and took off.

"Belutha!" Maybell ran after us a bit and stopped.

I turned to Rodney as we drove away, "When I say go, go!"

Rodney shook his head. "You're yellin' at me, an' we ain't even had sex yet!"

As we drove in silence I thought: This is a shitty start, but so what? We're just going to have a shitty ending.

The Mighty Man loved the Texas Panhandle. If he took 90 out of Van Horn, he could sometimes go hours without seeing anyone on the road. Of course, that meant no one on the road saw him either, so to my mind that was win-win for all. The closer he got to the Mexican border, the cheaper the motels became and the hookers he brought to them. Oren was nothing if not economical.

He was in one such place and his lover of the hour was in the bathroom washing up after sex. Or maybe she was wetting her face before sex, trying to work past her revulsion. I'm not clear which it was.

Oren sat on the edge of the bed, flipping channels on the remote. He was looking for something kind of sexy. The definition of sexy for

Oren was pretty broad and might include a slasher movie. I guess the pickings were slim because he went low on the dial to where the local stations were. And on one of them he stopped suddenly and stared at a news story. The setting was Maybell's Diner.

"A lone gunman—or gunwoman—took aim at the diner during breakfast. Her target is believed to have been Bill Bill, the diner's famous cook, known for being able to mind-read . . ."

Hearing Bill's name and seeing the police tape around Maybell's, its windows shot out, did something to Oren that I would not have expected. It caused him to feel protective. Not toward me, for sure. Not even toward Maybell. Just in general. It's a feeling guys rarely have, since most of the time they're just thinking about themselves.

Oren knocked on the bathroom door and told the woman inside there was something he had to do. He added a bit of extra twang in his voice when he said it. The fact is, she'd gotten her money and couldn't have cared less. Oren packed his bag, which never took more than half a minute, and went out to his Harley. He kicked the engine and looked out into the empty night.

He enjoyed feeling like a man with a mission.

By the time Rodney and me got on the highway it was nearly five p.m. In two hours of driving I don't think I said a word. The road was plenty loud for me. Every minute in Rodney's truck put that much more distance between me and Maybell. The further we got, the more I could breathe.

Rodney knew to let me be. Now and then I felt him look over at me. Some of those times I could tell he was uncomfortable. Some, I could feel him smiling, like: "I got her!" I don't think he was allowing himself to realize exactly what he got. Sometimes I pitied men for their sex drive. It got them into the worst situations.

We pulled over to eat when it got dark. The restaurant wasn't too bad, and there were rooms in a cheap motel next door, so we decided to stay. I paid for one room in cash. Rodney was behind me and I could tell by the sounds he made, the way he shuffled and moved, that he was excited, like his big moment had arrived. He wasn't a bad looking guy, and I knew he could have gotten sex a bunch of times over by now. But I had a feeling that he never went all the way because he was saving himself for me. Why any guy would do that, I cannot understand. But I was a little touched.

An hour or so later, I was staring out the window. There were few lights to be seen outside. This stretch of road was pretty deserted, and the restaurant had closed. Even the motel sign seemed dim. The longer I stared, the more I saw into the darkness. There was an outline of a mountain range far in the distance. A quarter moon gave the land a dim sheen.

I had lost track of time until I heard the shower shut off. After a few minutes, Rodney came out of the bathroom wearing only a towel around his waist. I could see his reflection in the window, lying down on the bed, shutting off the lamp. Now the only light in the room came from the muted TV.

I could feel his mind fixed on me, wondering how to get me into that bed. I didn't dislike Rodney, really. I mean I used to, for the longest time. But not now. His only crime was that he liked the wrong girl.

"It's not gonna happen tonight, Rodney."

That was all I said. I didn't even turn my head. I heard him sigh, then silence, then the bed squeaked as he reached for the remote. He

turned up the volume. A news story was on about the shooting at Maybell's Diner.

Many times after that night I thought of what my life would have
turned out like if he hadn't done that.

In the Hadley 8, Martin had gotten into his pajamas and sat on the
edge of his bed when he heard the knock. Even now, at this advanced
stage of his illness, he wouldn't walk barefoot across the carpet of a
strange motel for fear of picking up a fungus. He put on his slippers
and opened the door.

Rose came in without asking permission. She seemed restless and
paced around before saying anything. Martin closed the door and
waited patiently. Finally, she turned to him.

"I was scared, Martin. Can you understand that? Watching your
husband die, I don't think there's anything worse in this world."

Martin nodded. "I understand."

"Were you ever married? Maybe you *are* married, I don't know.
Did I make a move on a married man?"

"No. I was never married."

"Are you a gay?"

"Uh-uh. I just—Well, the truth is, women weren't exactly throwing themselves at me. I suppose I could have been married a couple of
times."

"What happened?"

Martin hesitated. Rose's question brought him right back to that
door he'd spent the last few days trying to avoid. He had a moment of
panic and wondered about the etiquette of running away from your
own motel room. But then he noticed something felt different about

it. The stench from that closed off place seemed to have dissipated. Maybe it was because of the shooting. Or seeing Bill in the police station, looking so lost. Then Martin had a new thought: perhaps that door had been open just wide enough and long enough to let the old air out. The shock of it was gone. Martin felt like he could open it the rest of the way and look inside.

And that's what did. He looked back into his past, to the handful of women he had managed to date, here and there, in his mostly lonely life. He saw their faces, back through the years, as far back as his twenties. And then he saw the face of the first woman in his life. His mother. He saw her more clearly than he had in decades. He could see how she kept her distance, even when she was in the same room with him. And how deeply he felt then that he displeased her. She never said that, and in hindsight he didn't believe it was true. But he believed it as a boy. He was sure of it.

It's why he kept to his room. It was why he chose books. And after that a life of ideas and theories and philosophy. Because he knew that in none of them would he ever find a disapproving frown or a reason for someone to decide that Martin was no one to love.

He let out a breath as the truth of it, the sadness of it, the reality of a life not really lived washed over him. For Martin had nothing left, inside himself or out, to keep himself from seeing what his life truly was.

He felt the hot tears running down his cheeks. "I think," he said softly, "my whole life has been nothing but one big hiding."

"What were you hiding from?" Rose asked.

Martin looked at her. The answer was so obvious. All these years he believed he was a smart man. How could a smart man not have known this?

"Pain," he said simply.

Rose nodded. She took his hand and led him to the foot of the bed. She sat down next to him. "The way I see things now is different than before," she said. "I know all this, it isn't forever. Even when we're young, nothing's forever. Tomorrow doesn't matter. Not really. Only now."

Rose leaned in and kissed Martin on the lips. This wasn't like those two kisses before. It was lingering, loving, and sensual.

There was a silence. Martin looked at Rose; her crystal blue eyes and the way her skin was taut over her cheekbones. He realized he had never seen a woman as beautiful. Gently, he leaned forward, and they kissed again.

Rose shook her head. "How come you gotta be at the end of your life before you have sense enough to enjoy it?"

They kissed and embraced, falling back together on the bed with a grunt.

"You okay?" Rose asked.

"Yeah. You?"

"Yeah."

When Bill woke up, he realized again that he had simply been unconscious. He vaguely remembered some strange images and events. Some of them seemed to happen to another person or in another life. Bill realized these were dreams. He knew dreams happened most every night for those with a lifelong commitment to a body. They provided a few hours of relief and recalibration. To Bill, it was further evidence of his fall.

He could barely remember what it was like to float. He felt weighted down by the trillions of cells working furiously to form and reform his body every moment.

Breakfast in jail was warm coffee, microwaved eggs and bland white toast. It was the first time Bill ate food he didn't like. It made the whole world seem even grayer.

After a while, his cell door opened. Chief Munt came to fetch him.

"Peter? I mean Bill. Time to go."

Bill stood. He was a prisoner now. In that body. In that life. He moved slowly, doing what he was told. That's what prisoners do.

The Chief held up a pair of handcuffs. "I don't think we're gonna need these, do you?"

Bill shook his head.

Munt held the door open. Bill followed him out.

In the police parking lot, Munt unlocked his squad car and motioned for Bill to get in the back. Bill obeyed. Going around to the driver side, the Chief put his hand on the door handle when he felt something hard and small on his back. He stood up straight, but he didn't turn. He knew not to.

"Keep your hands low where I can see 'em," Maybell said. She took the FOB from the Chief's right hand and pulled the gun from his holster.

"Maybell," the Chief said evenly, "That better be a spatula pointed at my back."

Maybell kept her gun where it was, pocketed the FOB, and tucked the Chief's service weapon in the back of her jeans. "Bill," she called. "Get out."

Bill got out of the car and looked at Maybell with a kind of dumb expression. "What's going on?"

"I'm getting you out of here." Maybell turned to the Chief. "Whatever that other guy did, Peter, Bill's no criminal. And he sure as shit ain't going to jail!"

Bill and Chief looked at each other. Both were surprised. Bill turned to Maybell. "Really?"

Maybell nodded. "Get in the truck."

With a look of apology to the Chief, Bill stepped away from the squad car.

"Maybell," the Chief said. "I don't imagine you've thought this through. You're not gonna keep Bill out of jail, and you're just gonna get yourself in a pile of trouble."

Bill turned to Maybell with a look of concern. "You are?"

"Get in the truck, Bill."

Before he could do that, a car pulled into the lot. It was a sky-blue Oldsmobile Cutlass. Maybell kept her gun low until she saw Martin driving. Rose pushed open the passenger door, which took some doing as it was nearly as heavy as she was. She held a petite handgun.

"Rose," Maybell said. "What the hell are you doing?"

"We've come for Bill. Right, Martin?"

Behind the wheel, Martin nodded. The night before he and Rose had made love, breaking a decades-long dry spell for both. Martin didn't tell her, but the exertion had put him on shaky ground, and the shaking just wouldn't stop. His skin was ashen, and his breathing was uneven.

The Chief frowned. "Rose, it's a little late in the game to be starting a life of crime."

"Go home, Rose," Maybell said. "I got this."

"We will not! We're bustin' Bill out! C'mon Bill, get in."

Bill turned to the Chief, as if for permission.

"Don't look at me. But I will say this. If you don't want your friends to get in trouble, I suggest you get in the squad car. Ladies, please put the guns away and let me do my job."

That was around the time that me and Rodney showed up. Rodney was enjoying the drama of it all. He skidded to a stop in the police parking lot, raising a cloud of dust. I got out and cocked my rifle.

"Bill, get in the truck!"

The Chief sighed.

Maybell turned to me. "Belutha, what the hell are you doing here?"

"Rodney," I said. "Tell Maybell I'm not talking to her. I'm here for Bill."

"*We're* here for Bill," Rose said.

"Go home, Belutha!" Maybell ordered.

"Rodney, tell Maybell she's not my mother anymore. Tell her she's fired."

"I'm not gonna tell her," Rodney whined. "She's standing right there."

Bill stepped up to me, and I could see he was still hurting from yesterday. "I thought you were mad."

"I was," I told him. "I'm sorry I hit you. But it wasn't you I'm really mad at." I pointed at Maybell. "It's her. She ruins everything."

"Oh, right," Maybell said. "I'm responsible for all the pain in the world."

"No," I said. "Just mine!" I thought: Do you really want to argue with me when I'm armed?

"You think you can do any better?" Maybell asked. "Why don't you give it a try? Go ahead, start having kids with Rodney! See how long he sticks around."

Rodney shouted from the driver seat, "Who said anything about having kids?!"

Maybell went on. "Why don't you try raising a family on your own. With no help! And while you're at it, try working twelve hours a day, seven days a week. You stay up 'til you can't think anymore 'cause a baby don't happen to sleep the same hours as you! And when you do go to bed, it's empty, 'cause no man wants a family that's not his own! Why don't you try looking in the mirror every day, knowing you're one day further from ever having love in your life again!"

I don't know how long it was that we stood there in silence. It was Rose who spoke up.

"Anybody else think we should continue this someplace other than the back of the police station?"

W e couldn't leave the squad car where it was. They'd wonder what happened to the Chief. So Rodney drove it behind the diner. I drove Rodney's truck, and we parked the three vehicles far enough down the road so we wouldn't draw attention to the diner. It was early enough that no one saw us sneaking around to the back door.

Maybell broke the police tape, and we went in. She hadn't thought to tell the bakery to stop deliveries, so we passed the smell of fresh bread in the racks outside.

All of us—Rose, Martin, Rodney, the Chief, my mom, Bill, and me—were crammed into that little kitchen. Rodney hopped onto the prep table and swung his legs. He was loving this again.

The Chief pulled Maybell aside, but he wanted us all to hear him. "Maybell, this is going nowhere good. Right now it's just me, and I will let this pass. No harm, no foul. But I'm telling you, and you better listen, someone *will* get hurt, and then there's nothing I can do."

The Chief looked at Bill, who was watching this intently. We all were. The Chief went on, "I like Bill too. I don't think there's a bad bone in his body. At least not now, anyway. But before—before what happened that night at the hospital, he committed a crime, and I'm telling you he's going to stand trial for that."

We all looked at Bill. Maybell grew thoughtful. She shook her head. "He didn't do that. Not Bill. Maybe that other guy."

"You don't—" The Chief shook his head. "You don't believe that nonsense in that article? Maybell, you're staking your whole future on a—a fantasy."

"I know Bill. I know who he is. That's not a fantasy."

That was the first time in my whole life that I ever liked Maybell. I hoped it didn't show on my face.

Bill stepped forward. "What will happen to her?"

"Well, Bill," the Chief said, "As you might imagine, interfering with police business, armed assault, kidnapping—these are serious crimes. Maybell, Rose, Belutha, Rodney . . ." The Chief turned to Martin. "I'm sorry, I don't know your name."

Martin was leaning against the sink, and it was an effort for him just to pass air through his throat to speak. "Martin . . ."

The Chief nodded. "All of them are in serious violation of the law. These are crimes that come with heavy penalties."

Bill looked around at us. His head shook slightly. "Why? Why would you do that?" he asked.

"Shit on a stick, Bill," Maybell said. "We goddam like you."

Rodney pumped his legs a little higher. "I'm just havin' fun."

Bill looked at the rest of us. I could see his mind working. He was surprised. He was touched. But when he looked back at the Chief, I knew Bill had already decided he was going to Phoenix with him.

He had started to say so, when there was a loud crash from inside the diner.

It seemed like we were out of time.

Gumballs we bouncing on the floor and I heard the sound of someone stepping on broken glass. We had all gone through the kitchen door and into the main diner before I realized there was only one man standing there.

It was Oren. "Hey, May," he said. "Sorry about the gumballs."

"Oren? What the hell are you doing here?"

"I saw the story on TV. Someone's goddam shootin' at ya?" He looked at the rest of us. "How ya'll doin'? Hey, Chief."

The Chief shook his head.

"We're kind of in the middle of something here, Oren," Maybell said.

"Hell, that's why I came."

"Oh," Maybell said. "So now you're comin' to the rescue, is that it?"

"Yeah, something like that." Oren pointed at Bill. "That's the sonofabitch who caused all this."

I stepped forward. "You leave him alone!"

"Hey, little daughter, I'm just tryin' to help you here."

"Did you just call me 'little daughter'?!" I was right in his face. I had left my rifle in Rodney's truck, and I was glad. I wanted to take him apart with my fists.

The Chief spoke up, "Let's keep things calm."

"That's right." Oren told me. "Like it or not, you're my daughter, and I'm here to help."

"No one wants your damn help, Oren. So why don't you kiss my little daughter ass on your way out the door!"

Oren had a line and I guess I must have crossed it. He stepped up and swung his arm back to hit me.

Maybell shouted, "Oren!"

His hand paused in mid air.

"I swear you lay a hand on her you'll be pissing out a rubber tube." Oren took a breath. I didn't take my eyes off his.

Maybell stepped up to Oren. "What the hell were you thinking, Oren? You come riding back into town like some kinda what—a hero?"

"That's what a man does. Back me up here, Chief."

"Jesus, Oren." Maybell looked down and realized she'd been holding a gun this whole time. She placed it on the counter. The Chief's service weapon was still in the back of her jeans.

She turned back to Oren. He seemed different to her somehow. Maybe it was seeing him in the diner, or because it was that particular day. The Oren in her mind and in her bedroom seemed taller and sexier and a whole lot smarter than the man standing before her.

Maybell took a long breath. "What the hell are you and I playing at?"

Oren was trying to find some response, but Maybell kept going. "I been working my ass off nearly twenty years tryin' to get you back. I'm ruining my life. I'm ruining my kids. And you know, I'm gettin' good and goddam tired of trying to look twenty-two again."

Maybell saw clearly what she needed to do. She was shocked at how simple and obvious it was and wondered, in amazement, why it took her so long to come to this. She looked Oren in the eye. "Whatever this is, it's over."

I'm pretty sure my jaw was open.

Oren took a step toward her. "May . . ."

Rose moved forward to block him. "You heard her!"

Maybell turned to me. To my surprise she put her hands on my shoulders.

"Baby, don't make this mistake. Don't go off with this boy. You do, and you'll regret it the rest of your life." Maybell turned to Rodney. "That's not a slight on you personally."

Rodney shrugged. I'm pretty sure he agreed with her.

Maybell turned back and looked at me squarely. "You got every right to hate me. I've been a terrible mother. All I could see was what I didn't have. I didn't see you. I am so sorry, baby. I am."

Maybell reached to put her arms around me. I pushed back hard. She lost her balance, but stayed on her feet.

"Baby . . ."

"Shut up! Shut up! Sixteen years you're the mother from hell. You think suddenly you can talk to me like you're a human being?"

"I know, baby."

I shouted louder than I ever knew I could. "STOP CALLING ME THAT! YOU'VE NEVER BEEN A MOM! NOT EVER! NOW YOU WANNA START JUST 'CAUSE YOU FEEL LIKE IT??"

I could hear my voice ring off the walls. The place was silent again.

"I'm sorry, baby, I'm so sorry."

Maybell tried to put her hands around me. I pushed them away.

"Don't touch me!"

"Baby . . ."

She reached again. I tried to push her back, but I was crying now and I didn't have any strength left in my arms.

"I hate you, Maybell!"

"I know, baby."

"It's not fair!"

"No baby, it's not fair. It's not fair at all."

I couldn't see past the tears. I had to lean on something and her shoulder was right there. I fell into it and started sobbing in her arms. I didn't know there was so much pain inside me, or that anything like it could ever come out.

I have no idea how much time had passed. I think I was pretty much cried-out when I heard, somewhere to my right, Rose's voice in a panic.

"Where's Martin?"

Earlier, we had all run from the kitchen and into the diner so fast that none of us took notice of Martin. He wanted to follow us, but his legs had stopped working. When he tried to walk, his knees folded under him, and he fell to the floor.

As we were yelling in the main diner and Martin lay there, his body was starting to shut down. Maybe it was having some time to himself that allowed that to happen.

Rose was the first to find him. When I walked in, Rose was kneeling by his head, stroking his cheeks.

"Martin," she said.

He looked up, relieved to see her.

"We need to get an ambulance," Maybell said.

Martin fought for the strength to speak. "The police . . ."

Maybell looked at the Chief and decided, "It doesn't matter."

She took his gun from her jeans and handed it to him, barrel down, grip forward. "You'll want this, Chief."

He took his service weapon and put it in his holster. "I need someone to call 911."

Rodney stepped up. "I got my cell in the truck."

"Go," the Chief said and Rodney ran off.

Rose held Martin's hand and he looked up at her. "I'm sorry," he said.

"Don't you dare, Martin. Don't you dare apologize. I wouldn't give up one tiny second of what we had. You hear me?"

Martin managed to nod. That was one weight he didn't have to carry anymore.

Bill knelt down to deal with the other. "Martin," he said. "Remember I said we'd talk when the time comes?"

Martin nodded.

"It's time," Bill said.

Martin understood what he meant. He was dying, not sometime, not later, not in theory. It was now. His face had the look of someone on a roller coaster, about to go down the steepest drop.

I looked at Bill and saw there was something different about him. There was a calmness, like I remembered from when he first arrived, when he was looking up at the night sky as if nothing in the world could touch him. He told me afterwards that state had returned because of Martin. Bill said that being around a birth or a death is the closest that humans come to the doorway to this world. At those times, it's possible for us to feel the other side. That's what brought Bill back to himself.

"Are you ready," he asked?"

Martin was too terrified to speak. He nodded.

"There's something I want you to do for me," Bill said. "I want you to close your eyes. And keep them closed. Will you do that?"

Martin looked right at Bill. Bill, who stood in the light at the top of that deep, dark well. Bill, who wouldn't leave him, not even now. Martin nodded and closed his eyes.

Bill leaned closer to make sure Martin would hear. "All of this, it was only meant to be for a while. None of us were ever supposed to stay."

Martin wanted to speak. He could barely contain his fear.

"I know it scares you, because it's an ending. And it is. But it's also a beginning. You can't see that from where you are. But I can help you see it, if you want."

Martin nodded.

"First, I want you to take a deep breath."

Martin's breath was jerky and shallow from fear.

"Good. And another."

Martin's next breath and the breath after that became a bit steadier.

"Now feel your body, Martin. Feel it lying there on the floor. Can you feel how tired it is? It's been working so hard, all your life. It never stopped in all those years. It's ready to rest now. Let it rest."

Martin's breathing stayed shallow, but it became steady. I could see the tension falling away.

Bill went on. "Not just your body. Your mind too. Your whole life, it never gave up trying to understand. It's so exhausted. You can let it rest now."

Rose held Martin's hand a little more gently. She didn't want to keep him there, anymore than she wanted to let him go.

"Keep your eyes closed," Bill said, "and tell me if you begin to see something."

Martin's face moved a bit. His breathing became troubled, and his body tensed.

"I'm afraid . . ." He was barely able to whisper.

"I know," Bill said. "Your fear's been working hard too. All it ever wanted was to keep you safe. It's done all it could. It's so tired now. It needs to rest too. Let it rest."

Martin's breathing steadied. It was so shallow, as to almost not exist.

"Look around you, Martin. Do you see something? It's okay if you don't understand it."

Martin gave the most imperceptible nod.

Bill leaned in right next to Martin's ear. "That's the beginning."

I don't know why, but I had a feeling that part of what Martin saw, maybe just a small part, was Bill. Not the Bill I knew, the one who was leaning over him, but who Bill really was. And if that's not weird enough, I thought that Bill was able to see Martin. Not the Martin we saw, but the Martin who was seeing him.

Bill told me later that, kneeling there, he became aware of that glowing string again. He followed it around the room. To Rodney, who had come back inside. And to Oren, at the kitchen door. To Maybell and the Chief. To Rose, on her knees crying. And to me. He said for a moment I looked right at him—not the Bill kneeling by Martin, but the Bill who was following that string. I remember looking away from Martin for a moment, but I didn't see a string or anything like that.

"There's just one more thing I need you to do," Bill said quietly. "With your eyes still closed, look around and steady yourself. And when you're ready, I want you to take a deep breath."

There was a quiet moment.

And then Martin let out his dying breath.

None of us spoke for a long time. The only sound in that room came from Rose's cries, muffled in Maybell's shoulder.

Who knows how long we would have stayed like this. The silence was broken by police sirens. After they stopped we heard a noise from the front of the diner.

Someone called, "Chief!"

"Back here," the Chief answered.

Deputy Kiplowski and another officer entered the kitchen door.

Whatever bubble we were in, it felt like a cold wind blew it to pieces.

Kiplowski looked confused. "Chief, what're you doing here? I thought you were on your way to Phoenix."

Maybell stood and looked at Munt. At once, we all remembered the trouble that was coming.

The Chief looked at Maybell and then over at Bill. He hesitated a moment, then he turned back to the Deputy.

"Kip, it turns out Bill isn't that guy Peter. It was a mix-up."

"But you said the fingerprints . . . the surveillance camera . . ."

"These things happen, Kip."

Bill stood up and looked at the Chief, who gave him the slightest nod. There was more noise from the diner. The other officer opened the kitchen door and motioned two paramedics into the kitchen.

"Fellas," the Chief said. "Let's get this body down to county."

They wheeled a stretcher over to Martin. Maybell put an arm around Rose to lead her away, but Rose wasn't having that. She had left the hospital room years before when they covered Jessie's face. She wasn't going to turn away now.

None of us did.

"Sooner or later, you're going to have to ask yourselves, 'Why?'

"Why a body?

"Why human?

"Why a new life?

"Why no memory from before?

"Why you?"

—*Bill Bill, Interview at Maybell's Diner*

Bill stared out the window and watched the world pass by. It reminded him of floating, in the way objects came and went, shrubs and cacti and hills. It was the landscape of a world he had wanted so badly to avoid. Seeing it now, on his last day, the beauty of it was overwhelming. Soon the open landscape would give way to suburban houses and then to city buildings. We were on our way to Phoenix.

Maybell was driving Rose's white Ford Escort. We thought about taking Martin's Oldsmobile Cutlass because it was bigger. I really think he would have liked that. But we had already broken enough laws that day and it was time to get Bill where he needed to go.

Maybell's eyes were on the road, but her mind was somewhere else. Maybe back at the diner. Even from the back seat, I could see that the way she held herself was different. I guess she spent almost twenty years of her life trying to will her body not to change. Today she gave herself permission to let that go. She seemed calmer now than I had ever seen.

Rose was quiet in the seat next to her. She had been mourning since her husband Jessie died. And now with Martin's passing, her mourning finally ended. The road was open and new to her, and it hadn't been either of those for years, perhaps never before in her life.

Rodney was sitting in the back seat, looking out the other window. He hadn't spoken since we left Hadley. Come to think of it, he hadn't said a word since Martin died. The experience had put him deep into himself, which surprised me. I didn't think Rodney had a place in there to go.

I sat in the middle, between Rodney and Bill. I wasn't clear on what we were doing. Bill didn't say much after the ambulance took off with Martin's body and the police cars left. We found him looking out over the road. After a bit, he turned to us. He took his time, looked at each of us. Then he said he had something that he needed to return. He asked the four of us to go along. I knew in that moment this would be my last time with him.

I was looking out the front of the car as we all sat in silence. I could feel Bill turn away from the window and look over at me. What happened next is almost impossible to explain.

I felt his thoughts inside me. At least that's what it seemed like. Not in my head, exactly. Just, inside. And it's not that I heard his thoughts. I just knew they were there.

At first his thoughts came all at once. Let's say that instead of running a movie over two hours, you were to run the whole thing in one instant. It was like that. And too overwhelming for me to understand.

But then his thoughts started slowing down and I could pick out a few. They were still happening too fast, but one thought spoke louder than the rest. It was Bill asking me to close my eyes, like he had that night when I was standing at the stove to guess Rose's order.

I figured I was probably just imagining this. But at least I wouldn't look too dumb if I closed them.

That must have made a difference because I began to hear his voice clearly inside me. I heard: I'm going to put my hand on yours, so you'll know this is real.

I felt his hand rest on mine. My heart started beating fast. This was just too damn exciting. I was a hundred percent certain I hadn't heard him with my ears.

Next, Bill said that because he was speaking thought to thought, I would be able to understand things faster. That was in part because they didn't need to go through the slower route of thought to mouth to ear and so on. But it was more than that. He said parts of the brain that process speech were slower than other parts. And now he could communicate with the part of my mind that worked almost as fast as actual thought.

I tried to understand this, but he said that the part of my brain that was trying to understand wasn't able to. So he told me to let go. And as soon as I heard that, I felt myself floating inside myself.

I could see there were thoughts taking place inside me; my thoughts. I knew what they were saying, but I didn't feel pressed to pay them much attention. I just let them be.

Then I felt a fear, of nothing in particular, just of the unknown, I guess. I tried to will it away, but I couldn't. The more I tried, the deeper it grew. I felt my heart starting to blast away inside my chest. I think Bill knew it, because in the next moment he gave my hand a squeeze and my heart started slowing down to normal. The fear was stopping.

I could hear Bill again. Only this time it wasn't in thoughts that spoke in individual sentences, but in whole concepts. If a thought was like one patch of color, Bill spoke in complete pictures. He told me about the thin glowing string. And how when he would mind-read orders, he followed that string to all the people in the diner. He told me—again this was not in words, but in concept—how he had been using that string to listen to others. And that now he was using it to speak to me.

I could see in an instant how it had worked for him in the diner. I could see that string going every which way to all those people, showing Bill all those lives and all those needs.

As I sat in that car, I felt like I knew, all at once, everything there was to know.

I knew the story of Bill. And Maybell and Rose and Martin and pretty much everyone around us.

I knew things I couldn't know.

About people I didn't know.

About things that, until that moment, I would have thought impossible to know.

Bill told me to follow that string with him to Maybell. So I did. I felt for a moment like I was inside her, the way Bill was inside me. Her thoughts were slow, almost painfully so. But her desire came across faster and I could feel it and understand it. It was a ferocious determination to never let anything harm me again. And because it was Maybell who had harmed me most, I could feel that ferocity aimed toward herself. The impression I got was that she was growing new muscle in herself, somewhere in her mind, right there while we all sat in silence.

And I knew she was doing it out of love for me. I felt tears deep inside myself.

The glowing string led me out of her and instantly everything became foggy. I heard Bill say to my mind that the string wasn't confined by "when" anymore than it was by "where." In other words, it could move forward and back in time.

He showed me a moment from before, three days ago at the diner, when I was sitting at the counter with my eyes closed and sensing a future me in that car. The diner became completely real, as if I were in both places with no time or distance between. I wanted to stay and talk to my younger self and tell her everything that had happened. But I could feel a tug in my mind. Bill told me to let go, and I did.

I began to see walls and objects and people walking by. It wasn't clear enough to make anything out at first. Then I realized these were things and people you see in a hospital, like gurneys and orderlies.

The string led me to a room where a doctor and a couple of nurses were standing over something, trying to make sense of it. They were looking at a man's body on a gurney, wondering how it got there, wondering who was to blame for not reporting it. The man on the gurney was Bill. This wasn't weeks ago, when Bill first got here. This was Bill from later today. He was dead and staring straight up.

I felt a wave of sickness come over me. I thought it would drown me. But before it could take hold, the string led me out of there.

Things started to come faster now.

I was in Maybell's Diner. The place had been put back together after the shooting. There were no more crowds. Just locals. I could see Maybell at the grill. She was cooking. Rose was back in her waitress uniform. She stopped by the grill with an order and put it on the spindle. Rose took a couple of prepared plates to bring to a table. What struck me most was how at ease she was now, like this was the Rose who was waiting to happen all those years she spent being the old Rose.

Things went foggy again and then I saw the string. It was showing me an intimate moment and it was a little harder to see. I got the impression that even the string wasn't allowed to look at this too closely. I was able to make out Rodney's face. He was older now, maybe in his mid-twenties. If I hadn't seen that side of Rodney, that deep side staring out the car window, I don't think I would have recognized him here. That deep part had taken root and was pretty firmly in place now.

I knew at once why I wasn't allowed to see much. Rodney was making love. I couldn't see who he was with, and I knew the reason I couldn't was that he was with me. Even though I couldn't see me, I was able to feel what I was feeling then, that future me. To my astonishment, it was love.

And then the fog again. Followed by some quick glimpses.

Maybell and Rose cheering at a softball game for a young man, stepping up to bat. His face was new to me, and at once I realized it was Sonny Boy. He was in his twenties. All the baby fat was gone. His eyes had a cleverness to them now. All he needed was time away from that house to come into his own.

Then I saw a teenager coming out of a school, my high school, arms linked with his girlfriend. No way I would have recognized Clover, and yet I knew it was him. Whoever his father was, he must have been a good-looking guy, because Clover was hot.

Then, more fog. That's what I assumed it was. Until I realized it wasn't fog at all, it was a bright light. I heard someone screaming in pain, a woman. I realized I couldn't see her face because it was me. I was able to see a doctor down at the foot of my bed. And Rodney, dressed in a surgical gown to my right, holding my hand. Maybell was on the other side, also in a surgical gown. There I was, seeing the future in some kind of mystical vision and the thing that struck me as most odd was that I would be okay with Maybell being there for this moment in my life. I figured that whatever was going to happen down the road, Maybell and I were going to be working out a truckload of issues.

The me in bed was screaming bloody murder until finally, suddenly, I could sense the pain subside. There was some activity at the foot of the bed and then the sound of a baby crying. After a few moments, a nurse came and put the baby in my arms, the future me. I could see the baby clearly, a boy.

Another nurse with a clipboard came to the bed and asked, "What's your baby's name?"

I heard my voice answer: "Bill."

And then I felt the whole world collapse in on itself, like a bathtub draining all at once. That thin glowing string traveled all the way back to the car. I heard a gasp from my throat and found myself in my body, next to Bill. I opened my eyes and looked over at him.

Bill was looking at me. He had a question on his mind. I could see it clearly in his face. He looked tentative and he also looked scared. I knew then what he was giving up. He wasn't going to remember any of this, not me, not being Bill, nothing. He was going to become someone for a while, someone who had never existed before. And none of this would come back to him until after he was done.

I suppose there's nothing as scary as the unknown.

I put my hand over his and I held it tight. The gesture surprised me. It was maternal.

"I'll take care of you Bill," I said. "I promise."

Maybell pulled over outside a hospital in Phoenix. It was the one where Peter Swaine was taken with an opioid overdose, just over six weeks before. Bill got out and closed the door.

He stood outside the car a few moments.

Then without a word, he turned and walked into the hospital, as if it was just a moment like any other—not an ending. Or a beginning.

End

ACKNOWLEDGMENTS

Over three decades this story has had many aunts, uncles, cheer-leaders and godparents. Among them: Jo Berman, Kevin Segalla, Elizabeth Browning, Will McRobb, Chris Viscardi, Catherine Stone, Nancy DeLucia, Jon Levin, Matthew Snyder, Alan Riche, Michael Besman, Barry Rosen, Jim Strader, Keya Khayatian, Louise Ward and Russell Hollander.

Heartfelt appreciation to David Wilk for using his vast publishing expertise to give this story a home. Thanks to Barbara Aronica-Buck for introducing me to David, and for her beautiful work on the cover and layout. A huge shout out to Emma Sweeney, my former literary agent, whose insights guided me to fill out the story. Thanks to Kitty Florey for her meticulous copyediting.

Appreciation to Susan Gorman, who set me on the path. To Emmanuel, who lit the way with the steady help of Pat Rodagast and Barbara Azzara. And to Bill Misener, whose lessons and tools are still with me.

Thanks everlasting to my parents, whose support for this project, my career and my life never once took a day off.

And finally to my remarkable, beautiful and brilliant wife, Lili —thanks for co-creating our life. These days are fun and loving and worth the long journey it took to find each other.